Sweet Summer Rain

By

Carol Nichols

The Seasons Series

SWEET SUMMER RAIN

Copyright 2022

All rights reserved

A Different Season

Mist of the Moment

Sweet Summer Rain

Wind of Change

Nichols Now books may be ordered at Amazon.com or contacting

CarolNicholsAuthor@outlook.com

Or

www.adifferentseason.com

Cover photograph courtesy: Richard Fogg

ISBN- 979-8-218-08710-4

Forward
By
Chris Nichols

"Hi Mom, how are you today?"
"I'm okay, how are you?"
"I just thought we could talk a little while."

My sweet child was wanting a distraction to help him work through his pain by keeping his mind occupied. We would talk for a couple of hours and every minute I watched tick by I knew would be a minute I would cherish in the future. Oh, how I miss that voice.

I love you, son.

ACKNOWLEDGMENTS

With much appreciation and thanks to…

My sister, Janice Southwick, for always believing in me and being the first to read each manuscript. I love you!

Eilene Gibbens, editor extraordinaire. Love and hugs!

Andrea Foster, editor/author. After reading a page and a half of my first book gave me the positive words which spurred me on by saying, "I can't wait to see where this goes!"

Richard Fogg, my attorney and friend is a phenomenal photographer who generously shares his talent.

CONSTANCE LOUISE SINCLAIR

A light chill resonates, even though it is nearing summer. There are not many things that hold power over Connie, but the one that does captivates her. Connie knows she will never tire of rain because, you see, it has a comforting, peaceful, settling feeling that calms her soul. Yes, gentle rain is God's way to cleanse and rejuvenate all things.

The feeders lie in wait. Absent are the cardinals, blue jays, dove, and sweet little sparrows. But not the robin, no the robin marches to a cadence all its own, aptly turning its head waiting for the subterranean movement of the lowly earthworm, a feast beyond measure. Yes, robins love the rain just as much as Connie does.

Connie stares at the bench, where in prior days, she and JJ made amends and avowed a new start. If only the sweet summer rain of that day could capture them in that specific moment, that moment where another resolution has been reached to never resurface.

Once again, Connie has given their fragile relationship to God, because heaven knows, even this gentle rain could quickly engulf them, erasing whatever growth that has been obtained.

Connie thinks of the tranquil drives she and Charles would take, letting the droplets encase them in that instant that so fleetingly disappeared. You did love our drives, Charles didn't you?

Connie, in a Scarlett O'Hara moment, relegates her thoughts to another day, another day, Lord.

Connie sees JJ's reflection as he slowly moves forward to startle her.

"No, you don't!"

"What?"

"You know what!"

JJ shrugs as his increasing smile is evident.

"You love to scare the bejeebers out of me."

JJ pulls her into him. Connie sighs, and willingly accepts his masculinity that provides a sense of normalcy long missing, and safety from the dangers she and Rosie seem to attract.

"Guess who called?"

BAPTIST HOSPITAL
Oklahoma City

The echo of footsteps draws near. My wayward mind bursts to attention. I stare at the waiting room entrance. My heart lightens as I recognize the familiar cadence, yes the rhythm of his steps. A smile greets my lips in anticipation of what lies ahead. This is to be a grand moment, the birth of a child, not my child nor his. The vastness of haunting memories could so easily moisten my eyes, and lessen my enthusiasm. JJ enters, jubilant, insightful, and oh so perceptive.

"You're done. What did she have to say?"

"Well, Amanda is going to be able to come and shop for her wedding dress here!"

JJ's eagerness cannot be contained. Amanda, his niece, and only living relative is to be married at Sinclair Estate.

Connie, in a déjà vu moment, remembers at St. Anne's hospital when they placed her in the consultation room which said 'Immediate Family Only', how Connie thought, it might as well say, 'Charles' only family'. But, with a chuckle, how wrong was that? We now have Amanda.

"That's wonderful. So Doug agreed?"

"From what she said, Doug wasn't big on it at first and if he could find any way to arrange Magic's racing schedule he would be joining her. I told her she would like it here as everything is readily accessible. No long drives to pick up items or get to and from the airport."

"That is so sweet. I love 'love'."

"Amanda knows that we are at the hospital waiting for the arrival of Rosie and Pete's baby boy. I told her she might have to share you a little and get this, she can hardly wait to hold him. She giddily ask me if I had ever held a newborn and I said, "Yes. It was you, Amanda!""

"JJ? Was it like holding a little piece of you?"

"She was so beautiful, that little nose and the curls covered her head in small black locks. By day two Margaret had one big roll of hair from front to back."

Connie straightens in the stiff hospital seats, and waits for the effervescent feeling that always accompanies Charles when he comes to her but feels nothing except a slight tinge of remorse. Connie touches her stomach with empathy for her empty womb.

JJ continues, as the storyteller becomes prominent, but he is interrupted as the double doors open. They are waved forward.

Connie takes JJ's hand, "I can't wait to hold that precious baby."

4

"Knock, knock," Connie whispers as they enter.

"Oh Connie, come, come and look. He just finished his first time nursing. Look at that sweet smile."

Connie agrees as Pete holds his son.

Connie feels Charles' presence and wonders. *You know what this is like, don't you Charles? Or do you?*

Connie smiles, nods, and embraces the moment as she glances at JJ, and motions him over. Connie steps to Rosie's bedside. Pete cradles their child. JJ pats Pete on the shoulder. Pete inhales, heightening his stature as he recognizes the respect he is getting from this significant achievement. He feels the pride of a father with his boy, bigger, stronger, and oh so positive. What a paradox, big burly detective, gun on hip, a clash of temperaments for sure.

Connie feels Charles once more.

JJ steps back. "Okay, I know you have three names picked. What did you decide on?

Pete pushes JJ into a chair, forces a stern look as he hands his son to JJ and, verbosely states, "Meet Peter Christopher Roseman!"

"Amanda, I knew I would find you here. How's he doing?"

"He's a little stronger, I think. He has to be healthy so he can make the trip to Oklahoma for our wedding."

"I know. Miguel is bucket feeding him as he needs to be with his mother longer, but I think this California sun will fix him up."

"Let's hope. Her udder was so engorged the vet said we needed to pull Beauty off."

Doug smiles, "So you have decided that is his name?"

"Yes, it just fits him and matches Magic perfectly. Black Magic and Black Beauty. But Doug, he has to gain strength or our plans can't be accomplished and accomplished in time for our wedding. I so want this to happen. It means so much to me as Connie has given and given."

Doug's smile broadens. "You are really attached to Beauty aren't you?" *This will not be easy*. Doug makes a mental note to check with Miguel.

THE SINCLAIR ESTATE

"J, you want to go out?" Connie asks as she hands him a glass of tea.

Connie walks to the edge of the lanai, cold drink held close, relishing the late afternoon garden. She briefly closes her eyes, draws a deep breath, and nods. "I am so glad you were with your sister during Amanda's birth and to hold that sweet child within moments of life leaves me awe-struck. I have never done that until now. The anticipation I felt today of the miracle of birth and especially this birth with all the scary moments concerning their blood factors, but by God's grace a healthy boy cannot be overstated."

Connie's voice trails off as she turns, takes JJ's hand, and gestures, "Let's sit awhile. So many moments to this day, but I want to ask something, if I may?" Connie feels Charles.

"Ask away."

"Tell me about Amanda's birth?"

JJ with a clenched jaw feels his muscles tense beneath his skin as this is the last conversation he was expecting to have. *What is Connie asking?"*

"I'm interested. I know about Charles and your sister, Margaret's, early relationship, and Amanda's conception, but I don't know the rest. I suddenly have so many questions."

"The rest?" JJ's initial astonishment lessens, although he can't help but remember Connie in California with not a clue of Charles' hidden affair with his sister, Margaret.

Connie sits and runs her arm through JJ's. JJ's temperament softens.

"What I'm asking is whether Charles was with Margaret at Amanda's birth?"

"Connie, I...I don't know if...

"Please tell me."

JJ turns on the bench. They make eye contact. JJ searches for a sign, a possible clue to Connie's temperament. He only sees somberness as Connie folds her hands in her lap and looks down.

"Well, yes he was." JJ says with no intention of proceeding.

"And..."

"Charles came but it was late, well into the night. He flew in through the kindness of a friend's jet."

"That would have to have been Phillip Chapman or possibly the Driscolls."

Connie starts to inquire about Charles' mood but instead she lets her thoughts drift to Charles. *Were you a proud Father? Oh, Charles, I couldn't give you children but I honestly and wholeheartedly am glad you were at Amanda's birth.*

"Thanks for telling me, J. Earlier today, with that baby asleep in my arms, I had hoped so. You know, there was a time that I couldn't have made that statement, but now, yes now, I am truly grateful Charles was there.

Connie becomes silent, takes JJ's hand, and tightly contains it in hers. *What a blessed day, meeting Peter Christopher Roseman. Oh Lord, the look on Rosie's face as she held her son. Lord how I dream of the look of love between mother and child one day. Yes, may that be real for me.*

I have a secret dream of a life beyond tomorrow,
Of a treasured child, carefree with no woes borrowed.
Hold fast my precious dream, find your secret place
Where you can thrive and grow,
Without doubt heaving fears to and fro.
For that place, sweet treasured dream is captured tight
And held profoundly close with all my might
So nestle near to me as I pray
That you, special dream will thrive far more
Than in my heart, but in my arms someday sway.

DOUGLAS HARTLY

"Miguel, wait up!"

"What is it, Señor Hartly?"

"I want to make certain you understand the importance of having the colt healthy for our trip to Oklahoma. Miss Bordillon wants both the colt and Magic to play a part in our wedding."

"Yes Señor, I can do it. He will be ready and I'm to make the trip with you, si?"

"Yes. Okay, Miguel, I'm trusting you."

ROSIE REDMOND ROSEMAN

"Connie, are you busy?"

"No, you know I'm available anytime. JJ and I were talking about Amanda and Doug's wedding."

"Oh, yes the wedding. I haven't received an invite, we are invited?"

"Yes, of course. You and Pete will have something to reminisce over as it will be in the same location as your wedding although with different logistics. And I must say, you sound much better. So, I'm guessing you got some sleep last night."

"Yes, a little. There is so much I don't know. The entire night I just lie and watch Christopher."

"You and several of God's angels." Connie quips.

"He is a true gift from God. The miracle of birth, no one can prepare you for. I have felt him for all these months but when I heard that cry, the tears were unstoppable."

"Aah Rosie, my friend, you are making my heart melt."

Connie silently lifts a prayer of thanks to God.

"Why I called is I have news and nothing either of us wants to hear."

"A problem? Anything that I can do, you know I will."

"Well, Pete told me CID is close to deciding in our case."

"Who?"

"You know, the Criminal Investigation Division. When talking to Pete, I go silent at any mention of our being detained by that Kirby guy, because I hate to get a conversation started that could lead to questions. Pete doesn't know the full story about us being at Driscoll's and pushing the buttons that got us in this mess. Pete believes we were innocent bystanders and there couldn't be any reprisal on the weird guy's part. But you know what, Connie?"

"What?"

"I fear that Driscoll will have his hired goon try and even the score. I don't want something to happen and Pete is caught off guard because he doesn't know there is even a chance of retaliation from Kirby Kerman over the OK Sportsman land."

"So, this is a concern to you?"

"Well, yes and no, but Connie do you think Driscoll wants revenge?"

"I don't know. I know he wants the land and desperately but to what end I can't be certain. You should have told me how concerned you are."

"I just thought it was my raging hormones."

"Hormones or not, this is one worry I can take away from you. You just helped me make up my mind. I need to make a call."

"Wait, Connie. I know what you are going to say and you will deprive yourself just to give me peace of mind. You know what Phillip Chapman said when we were in his Enid office, about Charles telling him the value is in the land and we know Charles led us to the deed through his keys you received in the mail. I can't have you give up whatever value the land has just because of me. I just can't."

THE OFFICE OF RICHARD FLAGG
Attorney at Law

"Lynda, this is Constance Sinclair and I was wondering if I might be able to stop by this afternoon for a brief word with Mr. Flagg?"

"Of course!"

"Hello, Mrs. Sinclair. I'm just on my way to court. Is this something urgent?"

"No, Mr. Flagg. It's concerning the land north of El Reno and Matthew Driscoll's continuing need to push for some type of resolution. Has he contacted you any further?"

"No, nothing since the initial correspondence. Has he or a representative been in contact with you?"

"No, but Mr. Driscoll is using leverage to have the investigation surrounding me and my friend Rosie Roseman's detainment at the Sportsman club closed. Mrs. Roseman has just delivered her first child, and this has her on edge. Any type of stress is not beneficial for her right now."

"Mrs. Sinclair..."

"Please call me Connie."

"Very well, Connie, first names will suffice. Are you making a request that I negotiate an agreement with Matthew, due to your friend's circumstances?"

"No, not exactly. Rosie is adamant that I retain ownership but at what cost? I'm not sure I can live with the outcome if something further happens. I was just hoping you might have an idea on how to alter our circumstances."

"Yes, I can think of several alternatives. Let me run through several quickly. Then I will have them emailed to you for your consideration.

First, you can sell it to an individual, even Mr. Driscoll, but keep the mineral rights, which I'm not fully convinced he will agree to. Second, you can donate the land to a public entity and retain the minerals. Thirdly, you can divide the property into tracks of land and thus sell to several people. This would make litigation a little more difficult against multiple parties. I must inform you, Connie, that Matthew Driscoll has the means to keep this in court for an immeasurable length of time."

PETER ROSEMAN

"Danny have you heard anything on the video?" Pete questions as he swings his leg over the corner of Danny's desk and makes himself at home. Papers ruffle.

"Like what?" Danny quips while dislodging the reports now firmly impressed with Pete's pants logo.

"Tattoos, facial rec."

"Nope, no luck. Camera is too far away. Pete, you need to invest in a few security cameras."

"For a rental. Don't think so."

"So you're gonna depend on your neighbor to do surveillance for you." Then Danny in a flourishing tone, says, "Detective Roseman!"

CONSTANCE LOUISE SINCLAIR

Connie enters the great room which seems to be the centermost location for finding JJ.

"Where are you?"

No answer. "JJ? J, COME TO THE GREAT ROOM!"

Connie turns at the sound of a chuckle and glances up to the circular balcony.

"You don't have to yell."

"Well, how long were you going to stand there?"

JJ descends to the upper staircase landing.

"Is it my fault you are so easy to look at? What's up?"

"Rosie has been told by Pete that Matthew Driscoll is pressuring the Canadian County DA to close the case on our being detained by an unknown assailant."

"Detained isn't the word I would use, and an unknown assailant is also known as Kirby Kerman. What does that have to do with Rosie?"

"I've just spoken with her and this has got her upset. She knows that Driscoll wants the case closed, so he can take legal action against me to regain the Sportsman club. Also, Rosie knows that a lawsuit quite possibly could place both of us on the witness stand."

"You need to decide on the land. Either you give it back to Driscoll as he wants, or you follow the recommendations of your attorney."

"I know. I at first said I just wanted the land gone, as that is what has brought danger. But Rosie is adamant that Charles led us to the land and I should consider that."

Connie slowly exhales as JJ consoles, "Think it over, it's your decision, but now we need to get the surrey for Doug's and Amanda's wedding located."

"Yes, you're right."

JJ in an almost disgusted tone, says, "Finally, let's do this. Anything but sitting around this house. At least at the ranch, I had things to keep me occupied but here it seems I have no purpose."

Connie takes note of JJ's admittance of idleness as she offers, "You want coffee?"

"Yes, I'll grab a pad, and let's sit at the bar. I'll make you a diagram of my thoughts."

JJ with a mug in hand begins. But Connie lets his words echo off as she leans back and wonders where JJ"s admission of idleness will lead and hopes her concern lay idle.

JJ turns and says, "Are we going to do this?"

JJ intently continues. Connie fakes a smile as she returns to her wandering mind.

JJ says, "Great, okay, there is a small logistics problem but a temporary entrance can be squeezed through the back hydrangea bushes to the south of the stables, and by doing that, Magic will be here and visible the entire ceremony."

JJ's drawing comes to life as he says, "This plan just reverses Rosie's entrance and the kids can still be married at the arbor but on the backside. The food tents will be reversed also and be closer to the house for the caterers.

This will work as this places Magic in the exact place he needs to be to play his big part in their wedding. I need to get measurements on the buggy to verify I have the exact width I need." JJ chuckles and looks at Connie as he takes this opportunity to chide her. "Because I must save every precious bush you love so dearly."

"Connie, are you listening? Did you hear you might lose a bush by using the horse buggy?"

"Oh, right, we need to find that surrey. It needs to be restored?"

OKLAHOMA STATE PENITENTIARY
MCALESTER, OKLAHOMA

"This is a collect call from an Oklahoma State Penitentiary inmate, if you wish to continue press 1, standard billing will apply."

"Jake is something wrong, this isn't your scheduled time to call. They haven't hurt you again, have they?"

"Momma, no. Just good news."

"Oh Jake, you sound excited."

"Momma, yes, but I need your help."

"What? What? Just tell me, anything, I'll do it!"

"Oh Momma, I've been given an early out opportunity. I've had an offer and if I accept I can get out of this place sooner."

"Oh, Jake, that's so encouraging. What do you have to do?"

"A..."

"No, I don't want to know. If you can get out, that's all I care about."

"Yes, probation now. I don't have to wait three years. They will start processing it as soon as I can get employment."

"You just tell them to call your father and he will verify that you have employment here at the dairy. I can't wait to tell him. Ben, where are you? Ben…"

"No, Momma, this has to be only between you and me. If you tell Daddy he will insist I work on the farm. The dairy isn't an option for this early out."

"Then what is?"

"Connie's place."

"Momma, I need this to work out. You can do it, Momma, can't you?"

THE WILSON FARM

"Geri, you expecting Connie?" Ben asks as he enters the farmhouse from the front porch. "I see her truck turning in this direction."

"No, haven't talked with her in a while. You know she has a gentleman friend visiting from California. I'll start a fresh pot of coffee."

"Never mind, they passed. That must be who is driving."

Geri walks to the kitchen window and looks north as the truck turns up Selectman's drive and thinks, *Okay Connie, I need to speak with you!*

CONSTANCE LOUISE SINCLAIR

"J, what are you doing?"

"I'm trying to decide if I need a jacket to go look at the carriage. I've been online locating an appropriate business that could help with this. I'm tired of waiting. Let's get this going."

Connie again notices JJ's restlessness.

"You might ask Ben Wilson if he knows of anyone. There are people in Okarche that can do this plus it will be close enough to personally monitor the progress."

JJ walks to the window, sees the fury of the Oklahoma wind in the top of the solitary Mulberry, and snatches his jacket. "You want to run up to the Wilson's with me?"

"Yes, I will. Oh J, Black Magic will be grand pulling the white surrey carrying Amanda to meet her groom."

JJ, with a fluttery feeling in his stomach, says, "I'll walk her down the aisle and she'll be happily married."

Connie feels Charles' presence as Connie thinks, *I know you should be the one to walk your daughter down the aisle and not her uncle. I understand that Amanda is your baby girl, but you must approve of Doug because you were the one that hired him as Magic's trainer. It will be a grand day, Charles, just wait.*

Connie realizes that JJ is still speaking. "I wonder how this changes the plans if Amanda flies here. Doug had said he and Amanda have planned this wedding around Magic's racing season to end at Remington after a stop at Ruidoso Downs."

JJ places his arms around Connie. "What are you thinking?"

"Oh, I'm thinking, either way at the end of the day, they will be Mr. and Mrs. Douglas Hartly."

THE WILSON FARM

Geri runs her hand through the lilac bushes hoping this horrible winter hasn't taken its toll. She welcomes the cheerful sunny day. Geri glances over her shoulder as the sound from the drive reaches her and she walks toward the east gate.

JJ, without hesitation and not waiting on Connie's introduction, offers his hand, "Hello, I'm…"

Geri smiles, "I know, you're JJ, Connie's 'gentleman friend' from California."

JJ feels mild irritation with Geri's specific enunciation and uncertain nomenclature but at this moment he realizes that his halted, guarded dialogue in previous conversations with Connie has placed him in this position, so 'friend' it is.

"Is Ben here? I wanted to inquire about some Okarche businesses that might be able to help with repairs."

Geri shrugs passed the grain bins, "You can catch him up at the barn. He's doing some repairs himself. Connie, come on in. Coffee?"

Connie sits at the oblong table, and brushes her hand across the vintage piece knowing this was Geri's great-grandmothers.

"Connie, I'm glad we have a few minutes without the guys."

"Sure, what's up?"

"It's something I need your help with?"

"Go on! Is there a birthday? I'm all in with parties and I love doing surprise parties, but it has to be within the next several weeks before the kid's wedding."

"Oh Connie, as always, you're too kind but this is more of a favor and one I am completely willing and able to reimburse you for."

Connie raises her eyebrow and offers a questioning gaze as Geri pulls the tray holding the accouterments for their coffee. Connie leans forward and while she watches her coffee become a pleasing caramel color she thinks, *What could Geri want from me that would be so costly she would feel obligated to make payment?*

Just as her bewilderment evaporates so does the patch of sunlight on the wooden floor. Connie places the silver spoon beside her pottery mug and returns to the 'smile and nod' approach she uses when in an uncomfortable situation. They make eye contact.

Geri pats Connie. "I'm making you tense. Believe me, that is not my intention. I have always appreciated your friendship over the years. You have watched the boys grow into men and it's because of this and only this, that I feel comfortable approaching you with this matter.

The push against the large wooden door distracts Connie but more so Geri with a startling effect.

Geri, with a firm grip on Connie's forearm whispers, "We'll talk later."

JEREMIAH JASON PAIGE

JJ paces before the fireplace. "Friend, what does she mean friend." You don't suppose that is the words Connie has conveyed and Geri just repeated.

JJ feels a quiver in his stomach, a slight chill to his neck and he cannot shake the feeling of being watched. He turns slowly, his body fights his advances only intensifying his weariness.

There at the first-floor landing stands Connie. A complete reversal of positions, as JJ never misses an opportunity to watch Connie unaware. They both feel uncomfortable. She immediately notices JJ's quick false smile.

Not a word is spoken as Connie navigates the stairs being unnaturally silent, intentionally straightening her shoulders, along with her stance as she braces for what lies ahead.

Connie is the first to speak. "What is it? Something has you distressed or are you upset?"

"You heard what Geri called me."

"Yes, this isn't the first time you have felt the sting of opinions."

"Yes, your right, but you don't seem to notice. Is this the impression you are giving people?"

"Certainly not. I prefer to not give any type of impression, as my life is my business and I don't have to explain. What did you want me to do? Go into a day by day, moment by moment or night by night, detail of our living situation."

"Well, no, but…"

Connie turns her back, seats herself on the ottoman, and says, "This all can be altered. There is a bunkhouse."

"NO. It's so exasperating."

"JJ, I know."

"You know I adore you, and I never want you to feel used or degraded in any way. I would never do that to you, but it is hard to feel the bristle of opinions, and not feel any gratification."

Connie once again relents.

AMANDA BORDILLION

Doug enters through the sunroom and sees Amanda at the table surrounded by boxes. "You want some tea?"

"Yes, please."

"What's all this?"

"Connie thinks it would be nice to have a pic of mother at the wedding. I've found several with mother and Charlie and several that I'm in. What a strange time that was. Almost like a dream, looking at these and thinking of all the things I didn't know.

Doug sits and takes some photos from Amanda and with a smile says, "Amanda, your mother was beautiful. I know where you get your dark hair."

Amanda, with a chuckle, continues to sift through the photographs. "These are enlightening, each is a special moment. Each defines who I am, where I've been, what I've done, and who I was all through a flash of a camera."

"I'm glad you can find your way to smile over these."

"Doug, I look at these and feel no ill will towards Charlie, even though I didn't know Charlie was my father and at the same time, not even dreaming when he was with my mother that he was another woman's husband."

"I was so afraid you were still blaming yourself for the harsh words you said to Charles the last time you spoke and especially after he passed before you could make amends."

Doug, with eyes engaged, embraces her hand. "I'm proud of you. You've come a long way and now, with the beginning of a new life, it is our turn to make memories."

CONSTANCE LOUISE SINCLAIR

"JJ, you're not hearing me. Rosie is concerned about the Sportsman Club and the Kerman guy."

"Yes, I heard that."

"She fears for Pete and also Danny. Oh, JJ, she is so delicate, fragile."

"I heard that too, but I thought you had figured all this out when you spoke with your attorney."

"Yes, in a way. He gave me several alternatives and each has its advantages but after hearing you reveal the other day that you have no purpose."

"Who said I have no purpose?"

"You did. You said, at the ranch, you had things to do, but not here."

"Well, I suppose I do feel left out a little, but Rosie is the top priority. I think as long as there is a chance of the case remaining open you can feel safe. Of course, that's me speaking."

"But Rosie isn't feeling safe either way."

"Okay, Connie, out with it?"

Connie walks to the fireplace, and to lessen the shock before continuing, straightens an andiron. "I have been going through each scenario Richard has presented and I come back to the same conclusion."

"And that's…"

Connie lifts a book from the hearth and walks toward the bookcase. "With each thought, I'm intending to divest myself of the land as being the only acceptable conclusion, but then I aimlessly, with a nod, start over. JJ, I just feel as if I should maintain control but to what end? I can't do that to Rosie."

"Give her a little time, and then speak with her again."

"Rosie is frightened but at the same time adamant about me retaining the property Charles worked so persistently to reveal. I, at first said, I didn't want to keep the land and am willing to return it to Matthew Driscoll but now…"

"Now what?"

Connie moves closer to make eye contact, "I'm tired of trying to make informed decisions, even with an attorney's help. "Yes, I'm going to ask Richard to do a Quit Claim deed divesting the property."

"To who?"

"You!"

JJ turns from the couch, and stares into the depth of the fireplace as he is struck with unexpected feelings.

Connie catches her breath, wondering to which side of the spectrum JJ's thoughts have gone.

"Don't you see, this is the answer?"

JJ stands resolute. Connie walks and touches his arm to reassure him before continuing.

"The Quit Claim deed transfers the land to you. You would own the property. I feel relief just putting this into words and I want it settled before we get caught up in the wedding. I'm doing it."

Connie swishes her hands together signifying action is complete, deed done, and decision made. "See, problem solved."

JJ leans on the mantle. *What just happened?!*

FLAGG and FLAGG LAW FIRM

Lynda, this is Constance Sinclair, and could you advise Richard that I have decided the outcome of our last conversation about the OK Sportsman Club. I would like it transferred to Jeremiah Jason Paige. Yes, Paige with an I and both land and minerals. Please call when Quit Claim is complete and I will sign.

GERI WILSON

"Connie, did I call too early? Hard to tell if there are any lights on down there."

"No Geri, you're fine. You know, Geri, I never appropriately thanked you for all you and Ben did for me while I was in California and wanted to clear that up right now."

"No problem and we fell short on our part when that trouble erupted with Jake. Connie, I need to speak with you but not over the phone. Could I come up, when you are alone, maybe this afternoon?"

"I wish I could say yes, but the truth is JJ's niece is flying in to help prepare for her wedding."

Geri deflates to a stooped posture. Her optimistic hopefulness for a quick resolution vanishes. In a soft voice of disbelief, replies, "What fun!"

WILL ROGERS WORLD AIRPORT

Amanda runs to meet them, leaving her lonely piece of luggage precariously sitting unattended in the middle of the busy Oklahoma City airport. She shipped the desired family photos and meager remaining wedding items the previous week.

"Hello, baby girl," JJ exclaims as he does a circular up-lifting hug.

Connie greets Amanda with a kiss on the cheek and says, "How was your first flight by yourself."

"Not bad after I made the plane change. I was on pins and needles until that was done."

"Well, you're here now and won't have to do the alone thing again as Doug will be with you from now on."

"I know. Doug and Miguel are on the road with Magic, making stops for each of Magic's races. But it will be a slow journey to Oklahoma."

Amanda knows she has intentionally omitted the mention of Beauty being with them, but the surprise must not be revealed this early.

JJ recovers the luggage and leads the ladies to the exit.

Connie insists, "Amanda, please sit in the front so you can have the best view. It will be quick, but we promise to bring you back when we can enjoy it all at a more relaxed pace."

The impressive Devon Tower looms in front and to their right as they exit the airport on Meridian Avenue South and JJ relates an evening meal at the restaurant at the very top of the 49th floor.

The Oklahoma City Museum is on the right with a brief glimpse of a Dale Chihuly glass sculpture in the window towering several stories.

Oklahoma City Civic Center is on their left the next block and Connie tells of seeing Lion King, Phantom of the Opera, and the highly anticipated Hamilton.

After a couple of turns, Amanda notices the Pinkitzel on the left before they drive under the railroad trestle into Bricktown where the ballpark and a prominent statue of Micky Mantle appears.

The restaurants are numerous, Toby Keith's, Chilenos', The Mantle, Zio's, and The Red Door for a few.

The Bombing Memorial is reverently shown as JJ slows to a crawl at 5th and Robinson. They point out the restored churches and apartments as Amanda's astonishment rises to the surface.

The chatter ceases as Amanda reflects on her disbelief of the loss of life and nothing else is spoken until they turn west onto NW Highway and the many windmills and oil derricks are revealed on the horizon. The sheer depth of the now open prairie and the ability to see miles upon miles has caught Amanda's attention though still sullen.

JJ glances at Connie in the rearview mirror and back to Amanda. Connie recognizes his uneasiness and is first to speak, "This land goes back several generations to the 1800s when Oklahoma was still Indian Territory", but to no avail as Amanda tearfully lowers her head.

Connie releases her seatbelt, and moves to touch Amanda on her shoulder. "Sweetheart, what is it?"

JJ nervously inquires, "Do I need to pull over?"

Connie, with angst, says, "Yes, please. Turn in at the old gas station on the right."

Connie opens Amanda's door. Amanda stands and buries her head on Connie's shoulder.

JJ clinches his jaw and walks the length of the cracked weatherworn slab. He struggles with himself about Doug's loyalty to Amanda. He draws closer. He hears muffled sobs interlaced with the words, "I never thought of it this way. I never imagined it was to turn out like this."

Connie, with a glance at JJ, nods toward the car. "Let's get you home. You are just overly tired. It has been a lot of first for you today."

JJ opens the door. Amanda leans toward him and tearfully continues, "Uncle JJ, what are we to do?"

JJ's mind races, with every possible scenario, during the short drive to the estate.

THE SINCLAIR ESTATE

JJ walks toward the stairs as he sees Connie. "What's going on?"

"I know, I know, God love her."

"Is it Doug? What has he done?"

"Nothing, Doug's done nothing. I just think the sobering mood of the bombing memorial and then you turned west on HW 3 and the sun lowering. You know everything is intensified at night."

"Connie, you're making no sense. What is it with women…?"

"J, she has just been hit with, not to mention, brought to the point of viewing your lives as they are now, and what your lives can never be again."

Connie feels Charles. His protection of Amanda is evident.

"I don't know if you seem too comfortable here in Oklahoma or she realizes the sheer miles between you both for now and forever."

As JJ and Connie ponder, Amanda cries through the loneliness she never realized could be felt since the death of her mother.

"JJ, I spoke with Amanda last night expecting to hear my exuberant, joyful, and fun-loving girl."

"Was she still crying?"

"No, but it was quickly apparent that she had been. She tried to cover her sadness but not for long. I ask if she wished she was back in California but she denied missing the ranch."

"She seems better this morning when she came down. Connie and I were as quiet as possible and let her sleep well into mid-morning. She gave me a forced smile, hug, and kiss on the cheek."

"What is Connie saying? You know they had that tear-filled weekend with all that tissue passing at the ranch."

"Connie said the wedding plans will keep them busy and put Amanda in a happier state. I was going to call on the surrey today but Connie wants to wait so she and Amanda can be involved."

"Thanks, JJ. I'll call back later but this is one development I don't feel comfortable about. Not comfortable at all!"

AMANDA BORDILLON

"Connie, the chicken salad was wonderful and I see you don't need my help with cooking any longer."

"You are too sweet. This was not cooking, but more assembling," Connie puts her arm around the still seated Amanda.

JJ smiles, "Baby, just glad you are feeling better. You know you can tell me anything. Anything at all."

"I know, Uncle JJ."

JJ pauses as he notices the use of 'Uncle' has returned to the verbiage of his once independent niece. "I want you to know that if your feelings toward Doug have changed in any way or if you need more time to think, or have any misgivings in the least, the wedding can be postponed. Yes, postponed indefinitely."

"I'm just having a difficult time putting my feelings into words."

"I know baby, no pressure."

"Doug and I talk every night and that makes me feel better."

"Better about what?"

"Better, just hearing his voice."

"Better but not better," probes JJ.

"How do I say this? How do I..?"

Amanda pushes her chair back. Connie watches from the sink. "Amanda, no problem!" Connie feels Amanda's need for space.

Amanda feels the vexation of what, of her unmet needs, of the change in direction of her life, of this uneasiness. Was that it, this feeling? Yes, this uncalming feeling of firsts? Should she rein in her emotions or try to find the words that could convey, even with clumsiness this churning from within?

JJ rises and with a clatter, in an attempt to distract himself and force continued patience, awkwardly gathers plates while he states in a shaky voice, "I'm here..." then clearing his throat, says, "I'm here, Amanda."

"Oh, I've made everyone uncomfortable. It's just everything is..." Amanda pushes her hair from her face and fumbles to get the stragglers confined in her hair scrunchie.

"I guess this is the first time I've seen life, my life, and everyone else's life in this new context. You just seemed so comfortable in the car from the airport, as well you should and I don't begrudge you every happiness."

"It's okay, baby as JJ embraces her. It's okay."

She lays her head on his shoulder. "I saw the vastness of the country, the opposite of where we live and then the reality hit me. It isn't where WE live, because you're never coming home and then Doug has been gone. Altogether, I felt this empty cravenness place inside, plus the anticipation of a wedding, a wedding which will also be a first, as I have never been in attendance at anyone's wedding let alone mine, and will Doug be enough? Do I love Doug or only love Doug when we are all together as a family."

Connie chills as she feels Charles' presence and thinks, *I know, Charles I know. It must be heart-wrenching for you, also.*

"Enough, enough," JJ consoles, "Let it go, Amanda. Cry it out."

"JJ, is there any way I can speak to you and Connie together? I mean alone and together without Amanda hearing?"

"Doug, no, I'm not certain I feel comfortable hiding our conversation and I know I won't be able to withhold information if it is something Amanda needs to know."

"I appreciate that, but I'm concerned about Amanda and just need to talk."

"I'm able to talk now, so go ahead. What's on your mind?"

"No, just trust me when I say I need you and Connie. Please!"

JJ stares at the ground as his eyes narrow and he replays Amanda's disclosure from this morning. "Let me see what I can do."

"It's a beautiful day. Could I interest anyone in a short drive?"

"How short? Do we need to change?"

"No, you're fine, where's Amanda?"

"In the garden. She is loving it."

JJ smiles and says, "Well, that old bench is getting some good use."

"No really, she's not on the bench she digging in the flower beds. I found her a pair of gloves because when I'd go out she would be walking in the garden and then next time she is digging. She is so funny, most of the time she is carrying the gloves in one hand and digging with the other."

JJ walks to the sunroom doors, looks out on the lanai, and sees Amanda in the garden. "She's busy alright."

"Yes, thank you, Lord. I can tell you from experience this is the best therapy. Your hands are busy with mindless work and leaves you with only your thoughts."

"Connie, it's a couple of months before the wedding should we bother her."

"Bother her for what?"

"I was going to take you both to see the buggy. It's done! Or I can pick it up myself and then back the trailer in the far side garage out of sight."

"No. Let's just ask her. I haven't brought up the subject of shopping for a dress not to mention, cake, flowers, food…"

"Okay, should I toss my hat in first?" JJ cringes a little as he opens the door.

"You're so funny," Connie chides.

"Amanda, honey. You're really after it."

"Oh good. Connie come here."

"What?"

"Do you know what this is?"

"I certainly do. Blue Moon Lobelia, loves afternoon shade just like the Hydrangeas."

"And this?"

"That's sweet Alyssum. Smell it."

"Oh my. It smells wonderful like I'm baking with vanilla. I love these babies, what are they?"

"That's Aunt Elsie's wild violets and that's Aunt Louise's pink peonies."

Before Amanda got her next question formed, Connie warned, "Amanda, you are going to have to wait. Let me run in and get my garden journal. I can't remember all of these."

Connie turns and finds JJ on the bench with outstretched legs, his arms behind his head, and a gentle smile of satisfaction.

GERALDINE WILSON

"Connie, can I come down?"
"Oh Geri, sorry, no!"

"Connie, I'm calling you because I never heard back from JJ. What did you all decide?"

"About what, Doug."

"I asked JJ last week to find a time when I could talk with you both. I'm worried about Amanda. She seems...I don't know what to say exactly, she just seems a little off."

"Really," Connie says as she walks to the back door to see if she can locate JJ. "Doug, he's run into Okarche to pick up the surrey and it doesn't seem as if he's back yet. Amanda hasn't seen it as well as you, of course."

"That's nice Connie and I appreciate all you are doing to make this special for us, but..."

"But what Doug? You two are still talking every night aren't you?"

"Yes, but the first few nights she was with you were so tenuous, I began to question myself as if this was the best idea. I was never really for it. Being apart this long. I just wish she had made the trip with me and Magic like we first decided but it was all about wedding preparations and the dress. She was so excited about getting her dress. It makes me smile. She was excited wasn't she Connie? Connie?"

"Doug, we haven't gotten around to that, but soon. She's still getting settled in and feeling more at home each day. But did I mention that J is gone to get the surrey as we speak?"

Connie hears a long exhale as she steadies herself and quickly searches for words to not hurt Doug but also safeguard Amanda.

The silence continues as Connie rubs her brow to her temple.

"Connie, I wanted to talk to you and JJ both to get a consensus on what is going on with Amanda. I felt I could make a fair determination after speaking with you. But I was wrong."

"Wrong, Doug. Wrong about what? You know I love you and Amanda equally."

"Connie, that is kind of you to say but I know that can't be true. You and Amanda have forged a relationship unequaled, even to ours."

"But Doug, I would never do or say anything that would hurt either of you."

"I know, Connie. I wanted your and JJ's opinion but now, I have made my own decision, but it will cost. It will cost all of us."

"Doug, JJ's here. JJ, Doug has me concerned and says he has made an independent decision as we never returned his call."

"Doug, don't do anything rash. I completely misunderstood your request to be heard but now..."

"No, JJ, earlier, I was going to fly to Oklahoma between races and leave Miguel with Magic. That way I could be with Amanda for a couple of days as I feel she needs me. I might be wrong, JJ, does she need me? Does she? No, maybe it's me needing her. Needing her reassurance only I can feel with her in my arms."

"That's perfect. When will you be here?"

"As I said, that was earlier, but now as I hear Connie speak of Amanda's resistance to continuing with plans for our wedding, I've made a bold decision that will cost not only you and me Connie but also Magic."

"Doug, what are you going to do? Magic didn't ask for any of this. He doesn't deserve to be hurt as he is only a loving and loyal companion and I must mention unwavering."

"Connie, I can't continue on this circuit with my life's future with Amanda in peril. I'm forfeiting Magic's remaining races which will drastically reduce his standings and even give rise to his abilities plus raise concerns about possible health issues. For you and I as joint owners, it will be a financial loss with future repercussions for now and next season. Magic is the big loser in all this."

"Doug, we can live with all that as can Magic because JJ and I both want nothing but you and Amanda's happiness. I should have never pressured you two into changing your plans. Never question that you all are meant for each other as your days together just made you love and appreciate each other more and more. This is only a little ripple in the road. Come home Doug and come quickly with our full support. We love you both."

"Are you coming?"

"Where," asks Connie.

"To find Amanda."

"You're not going to tell her Doug is on his way," Connie states as she is having to run to keep up. "That's not up to us. Doug will call, I'm certain."

"No, I'm going to ask her to walk with us to view the restored surrey. That will allow her to revisit her feelings and hopefully give me…a…us a little piece of mind as to their future."

"Promise?"

"Yes, I promise?"

"I'm here, in the garden. Come look what I discovered Connie."

"Wow, you've been busy after I showed you how to tell between the flowers, weeds, and ground cover."

"What is this? More blues and they look like they could pop almost like a balloon."

"Yes, I often refer to them that way also. The name is Campanula."

"Wait. Let me write that down."

"You've started your own garden journal. Good job!"

"Look, JJ."

"I see," states JJ as he leans in and feigns almost believable interest.

"Amanda, I have something I think you will like to see."

"It can't be more ponies as I haven't heard any trucks. Is it kittens? Did you find kittens in the stables?"

JJ moans as he believes if this surrey doesn't immediately show a pulse and breath that Amanda will be less than impressed. Not the outcome he was hoping for.

Connie stands by Amanda as Connie is also anxious as she has only seen the surrey in pre-restored condition. JJ opens the double doors which reveals the little white surrey in full side view. Both girls explode in excited laughter as they embrace each other. JJ cannot be more delighted and is almost to the point of jumping with the girls as his anticipation level is definitely at Defcon 4.

Amanda exclaims, "It has fringe."

Connie with her head bobbing in approval walks forward. "And brass nail finishing. It's just beautiful. Beyond words."

"And I'm to ride in this? It has two seats."

"Oh, don't worry about that. The backseat will be filled to overflowing with lots and lots of flowers. The only important seat will be the one you arrive sitting in and being pulled by Magic and all the guests will be seated over there by the arbor but you will be in full view all the time."

Amanda's face dulls slightly as she says, "It is beautiful," and kisses JJ and Connie.

CONSTANCE LOUISE SINCLAIR

Connie paces. "Well, what do you make of that? All that excitement at seeing the surrey and then the fizzle at the end."

"Where are you going?" exclaims JJ.

"To talk to her."

JJ races to head her off. "No, you're not. You made me promise not to instigate anything before Doug speaks with her, hopefully later tonight.

"What do you think is going on, J? Are we hosting a wedding or not?"

"Amanda, how are you feeling, sweetheart?"

"I'm, okay. Have you made it to Ruidoso?"

"Yes. Got here this morning."

"How is Beauty doing?"

Doug smiles as he feels the lift in her voice as she speaks of her colt. "He's wonderful. He runs, jumps, and kicks the minute Miguel releases him in the paddock. He is back to his healthy feisty self."

"Aah, send me a pic, I miss him."

"Just him? I know someone who would like to know he is missed also."

"I miss Magic too but Beauty is still a baby," Amanda states with a slight flourish in her tone and Doug hopes that is for him.

"Hey Missy, I wasn't speaking of the big boy."

"You weren't. Then who? Let me guess. Miguel?" Amanda explodes in laughter as she drops onto her bed and falls into the overabundant pillows.

"Oh Amanda, you made me feel so much better just hearing you laugh. I miss you so much especially after all the days we have spent together. It is like a piece of me is missing without you."

"I know. I'm sorry Doug. It won't be too much longer and you will be here and we can be together."

"I know, I have something to tell you. You know how sad you were the first few times we spoke."

"Yes and that's why I can hardly wait to see you. We can talk about all that and then see where we both stand on everything."

"Amanda, are you having second thoughts."

"How did you know Doug? Have Connie and JJ guessed? Oh my!"

JEREMIAH JASON PAIGE

"Connie, where are you? Just got a text from Doug saying he spoke with Amanda and is now loading headed this way."

"This late? It will be a long haul."

AMANDA BORDILLON

"Oh Lord, thank goodness it's finally morning. You know when I'm restless I just like to get up, eat some cereal and sit awhile but I didn't want to disturb Connie and the last time I looked the lights were still on in JJ's room…and that dream I had that woke me. My hand was in some type of liquid, I guess water, and my engagement ring just slowly dissolved and I was able to save but a small portion.

I'm famished. Let's go say good morning to the kitchen and take a quick peek in the garden.

Amanda makes her coffee and quietly steals to the garden bench. Hints of another day's beginning slowly, if not magically makes their appearance. She has serendipitously caught the birds as they awake. A robin takes flight from her nest. Amanda places her coffee on the table and tiptoes to glimpse the three blue eggs discreetly placed on the softly swaying bow of the towering evergreen. Amanda closes her eyes to let the sound of nature seep into her very being. I'm listening God.

Amanda hears the familiar chimes of the door being opened and sees Connie. Amanda, instead of feeling her serenity stolen thinks that Connie is a welcome interloper and offers a friendly, "Welcome and good morning."

"Good morning to you also, and good morning, Lord. What a glorious morning and no wind."

"I thought California was the only one with endless winds but guess not."

"Yes, seems the only time we have no wind is when a front is coming through and we get a few days' reprieve. Sometimes it's only a few hours but I'll take all we can get. The wind makes it hard on the water system's efficiency. It hasn't been needed for now as the Lord has blessed us with sweet summer rain."

"Do I need to water the garden with a hose?"

"Maybe. We will have to dig the hose cart out from where it has been stored for the winter. Let's walk in the garden. This is my favorite time to look at the flowers and assess their need."

"Okay," Amanda says with a lilt in her voice. "I have some questions."

"Oh my and me without my journal. The questions better be very rudimentary."

"No, no flower questions as I don't have my journal either. I just want to show you some spots where there isn't ground cover or flowers and was wondering if anything will be coming in there?"

"Good question. We will give it a few more days and then we can do some replenishing with new plants."

"Can I go?"

"Certainly, but in the meantime write in your journal the location and condition of the area where we will be planting so we can have an idea of moisture level, shade or sun, and the height, such as front of border should be short, middle should be medium and back, which will be tall."

"I can do that."

"Oh look, the bird bath is empty. Definitely, time to get the hose cart out and keep our feathered friends happy. But for now, I'm hungry. We haven't had a decent breakfast since you've been here. It has just been hit and miss. Come on, I've got sausage patties in the freezer. Let's have a big country breakfast I know you are used to."

"What's that smell? I'm offended, you weren't going to wake me?"

"Yes, silly, it's not time for the eggs yet. Biscuits still have a few minutes."

"Biscuits? 7Up Biscuits?"

"No, sorry didn't have the soda on hand so these are Pioneer."

JJ heads for the oven and hits the light switch several times to no avail. "The oven lights out?"

"I know. Silly thing. Watch this." Connie opens the bottom oven and the top oven light comes on. They all laugh.

JJ notices the overabundance of food. "Looks like you're cooking for an army."

"Either way, you have to make a full pan of biscuits. That's a cooking rule, I think," Amanda offers.

"Hey Sweet Pea," JJ says as he squeezes Amanda's shoulder. "You come to visit and we put you to work cooking."

"I don't mind. Reminds me of the ranch when Connie taught me to shop and I taught her to cook and now Connie is teaching me to garden and I will cook for that trade-off any day."

"You still have me beat on the cooking. You cook and I take shortcuts. Go figure," Connie quips as they all turn toward the sound of someone entering through the north entrance.

JJ walks swiftly to the back door and exclaims, "Well, I'll be," and then, "Amanda, it's someone for you!"

Amanda answers, "Really, are you sure? Connie, would you come and stir the gravy."

Connie walks to the stove, takes the wooden spoon from Amanda, gives the gravy a couple of stirs, and turns it off as she is not going to miss this encounter.

JJ opens the door, and steps aside as Amanda cranes her neck for a better view but is emotionally shaken, unable to advance. Her hands go to her mouth. Spontaneous laughter along with tears forces a step back. She leans into the doorway for support. As her knees go weak, she looks down and away to hide her emotion.

Doug slides from the rig, drops from the elevated step, and stands without attempting to close the door. He removes his cap and throws it toward the seat in a futile effort to save it from toppling to the ground.

Through a stony expression, he advances and with an unknowing heart takes one step then two.

Amanda in disbelief and with several nods, mummers, "Oh Doug, I can't believe it. You're here. You've come."

The steps between them magically melt as they fall into each other's arms.

JEREMIAH JASON PAIGE

JJ and Connie wait in the back entryway as the young couple, desperate for this reunion, speak words solely meant for each other. Nevertheless, the visual emotions of each, speak volumes.

Arms entwined they enter and as if on cue, they hear from the other room, the grandfather clock extolling the glee felt by all.

Connie grabs additional place settings as JJ returns from the hauler with an also famished Miguel.

Amanda seated by Doug not so gracefully jumps to her feet and hollers, "The gravy!"

Connie scolds, "I got this. You sit down. I turned it off when we went out," and then, "Oh my, it's cold and thick, very thick." Connie raises the spoon which shows an elevated hunk of gravy tenaciously attached.

Amanda, with a smile, instructs, "Turn it on, add more milk and find a whisk."

After the gravy's successful revival and hands being offered, Connie says grace.

"Our dear Heavenly Father, we not only ask your blessing over this food but also Lord, we are here with hearts filled with joy for your protection in returning Doug safely and securely to us. You know our needs before we utter a word Heavenly Father and we thank you for your grace shown to each of us and Lord, in all things we give You the praise, honor, and glory through Jesus' dear name. Amen."

Connie's voice trembles in her exultation to God as it so often does these days and her feeble attempt to control her heartfelt feelings is unsuccessful.

Conversation ignites as each one laments, "No, you go first."

Doug leans and whispers to JJ who rises and heads to the refrigerator only to return with Tabasco and salsa. Connie says, "Wait I have tortillas'." Miguel smiles, blushes, and gives a nod of thanks.

Amanda quips, "Doesn't it feel good having everyone together just like at the ranch?"

Everyone nods assent except JJ as he remembers Amanda's declaration of the fear of life alone with only her and Doug. JJ loves his niece but at the same time he would like the opportunity to continue his and Connie's journey. His thoughts about this happening quickly evaporate as the wedding is weeks away or his hopes for a wedding at least.

Doug stops eating, sits back in his seat, and places his arm loosely on Amanda's chair as the two men make eye contact until Amanda turns and cajoles, "I have a new love."

"Really," states Doug with peaked interest. "You have me concerned now!"

"Why," states Amanda with a hand to her chest to feign astonishment.

"Well dear heart, I know your first love is Magic and ponies placing me a weak second but now I'll be relegated to a slow third and quite likely won't even make win, place, or show."

They all laugh and Connie continues the conversation. "Oh you men, ladies can have many loves without placing numerical importance on each but Doug, if you want number one, you left out Amanda's and also mine, and that SHOES!"

Connie and Amanda giddily laugh as they clasp the palms of their free hands with an exaggerated shake as a sign of collaboration.

Amanda directs, "Speaking of ponies, let's get this food put away and go to the stables."

Connie adds, "You brought ponies?"

Amanda asserts, "Kinda'."

Doug speaks quietly with Miguel who leaves as the food is haphazardly placed in the refrigerator, dishes abandoned and aprons tossed. The ladies are enlivened. Amanda is eager to reveal and Connie, likewise, is eager to see.

They enter through the main portico which contains Magic's stall and first home. The home that Connie believed once, years ago, was his forever home before she was forced to place Magic on the auction block during the assets sale to try and save the estate from bankruptcy. The fire that Connie feels in her gut from that long ago time is quickly extinguished as she hears Magic's whinny as he once again presides as supreme ruler of his royal court. The ladies dutifully take their places, one on each side as he smells then nuzzles his loyal subjects.

"Oh Magic, I've missed you," Connie exclaims as she rubs her cheek into his, smooth as silk, mane, and neck. Connie begins to ask about his races but quickly coughs as she realizes Amanda doesn't know Doug has decided to forfeit Ruidoso but adeptly changes to, "You can now get some well-deserved rest before you prance this beautiful bride to meet her groom."

JJ changes position in an attempt to see Amanda's reaction to the bride and groom reference just as Amanda turns and blurts, "About that." All are caught off guard.

JJ glances at Doug who is chewing his lower lip as he steps toward Amanda and touches her arm. "About what, Amanda? About the wedding?"

"Yes, about the wedding and our escorts!"

"Oh, yes, you are completely right," Doug states after deliberately having to make himself take a breath.

Amanda impatiently cajoles, "Where is he?"

Doug lets out a whistle and the proud colt impressively enters from the far end of the stables.

Amanda, softly confides to Doug, "When did you teach him that?" and then as he approaches closer headed directly for Amanda and Connie, Amanda exclaims, "Oh Doug, I'm so glad you taught Black Beauty to come on command."

Doug reaches out and catches his bridle to stop the colt from barreling into everyone.

Connie, in awe, sighs, "Oh my, he looks like Magic, he looks exactly like Magic!"

A smile comes across her face as she feels Charles with her once again and thinks, *It's been a while, baby. You've had me worried. I thought you had left me but, Charles, I consoled myself with the thought that God must have you on assignment.* Connie rubs her arms to further enhance Charles' effervescent presence and as she broadens her smile, thinks, *Charles, you really must learn to multitask!*

Doug, on the same wavelength as Amanda, says, "Connie, there is to be two Beauty's accompanying my gorgeous bride to my side if little guy here will cooperate."

"Oh that will be perfect and you've named him Black Beauty?"

"Yes," Amanda smiles, "When I was first able to completely walk up to him. I said, 'Come here you little black beauty and it just seemed to fit him perfectly."

"Yes it does, Black Beauty to go along with and complement Black Magic."

They all agree. JJ walks around the colt and quickly concedes, "I'll have to agree with you Connie, he's Magic's double."

"What are your plans for this little guy? Think he has Magic's abilities to go along with the looks?"

"You talking about racing? I haven't given that a thought. He is the first Mustang baby we were able to break to the bucket and halter so the first one Amanda could love all over. We might look into that after he shows his temperament and abilities. It's not like you just say, 'Let him race' as it's all up to him. He has to have the all-out heart to grasp running because I won't use the whip as encouragement no matter what others say."

"Yes, we can wait and see. Never say never!"

JJ thinks, *Yes, never say never. Everything in life seems to accelerate at amazing speed. I wonder which lane this little guy will take. Shall we let life gallop us along taking us for a ride whether we want the ride or not! What is wrong with me? Pull it together.*

JJ has a convicting moment!

CONSTANCE LOUISE SINCLAIR

Upon entering the house Connie lays her sunglasses on the desk, removes her phone from her bag, and fumbles for her brush to bring her hair under control. Once again the Oklahoma wind with an acclaimed gusts of 48 to 51 mph is howling according to David Payne, News 9.

As she picks up her phone, Connie thinks, *I can't wait to show Amanda the water blowing out of the bird baths and fountains as she remembers telling a friend at a race in Pennsylvania, who was complaining about the small breeze gently moving her hair, that back home the bird baths would soon be empty due to Oklahoma winds.*

Connie's phone gently vibrates. Connie picks it up and sees two missed calls. Connie engages the voicemail feature as Lynda at Flagg and Flagg notifies her that the documents transferring ownership to JJ on the disputed land were ready for her signature.

Oh, good, glad that's handled, thought Connie.

The second message was from Geri and her voice seemed more than persistent even dire saying time is getting short, must talk.

Okay, the lawyer first then definitely Geri's problem.

JJ enters, the wind catches the door and with a loud bang, shuts abruptly. "Wow, sorry. Luckily that window didn't break. I'll help with the clean-up." Connie, who are you calling?"

"No one just listened to a couple of messages and great news."

"So tell me, love great news."

It's Lynda from the law firm saying that papers are ready to be filed at the courthouse after I review and sign."

JJ turns, "Huh?"

Connie replies, "Let's get the dishes in the dishwasher."

Amanda and Doug enter and busily join in. Within minutes the job is complete.

"Connie has to run into El Reno, I'll go but only if you two want to come."

Amanda defers to Doug but before an answer is given Connie says, "That's okay kids. I know Doug is tired and JJ and I will be back in a couple of hours."

"I need to go?"

"Well, not exactly but it would be nice if you would accompany me," as she glances toward the kids with a nod.

JJ silently agrees.

"Doug, please tell me you will stay in the house and not the horse hauler?"

"No problem this time around, I've had enough of the hauler, the house it is. A shower and a little downtime will be wonderful."

Connie tosses the keys, "You drive. This will give them some time alone and maybe Doug can pin Amanda down on her misgivings she has insinuated to us."

"I know, Doug said she implied as much last night."

DOUGLAS HARTLY

"I forgot to ask which bedroom I will be in!"

"I can help you with that."

"I can't say I have ever been any further than the kitchen area for an occasional meal with Charles and Connie during race season at Remington and then at Pete's and Rosie's wedding. I'll grab my stuff."

"You're going to be in for a pleasant surprise because this is the complete opposite of the ranch, not to mention the weather," Amanda gleefully confides as she adds a hop to her step to keep up with Doug's long stride.

Inside the hauler, she remembers the only time she has been in the main area. It was the night at the ranch she visited Doug to confront him with the allegations from JJ that Doug had insinuated she had pestered Doug to the point of impeding Magic's training.

Amanda sees the chair, lamp, and table where Doug had placed her glass as he asked her to dance. Yes, the night she felt his touch, the warmth of his body, and to be held in his arms and first feel the wild beat of her heart.

Amanda had never been held that way or even danced with anyone except being twirled between her momma and Charlie. The moment lasted that evening only because fate released calamity on them while havoc and chaos ruled the next morning when Connie visited the ranch to be confronted with the hidden truth of Charlie's life.

Amanda turns and wonders how long Doug has been standing at the end of the bar with his gaze fixed on her. His arms are laden with clothes both clean and soiled, a couple of hats and boots set at his feet. She grabs the boots and hats as she feels her face flush.

Back in the house, Amanda leads the way through the kitchen into the massive living area and left up the grand staircase.

"I'd prefer to sleep downstairs so I don't disturb anyone in the mornings."

Amanda turns, "Sorry, that's not possible. There are no bedrooms down here."

"All upstairs? None, even toward the back off of the kitchen?"

"No, sorry."

Doug's discomfort is apparent. "Never been much of a campus man, especially co-ed."

They continue towards the upstairs bedrooms. Amanda hopes Doug will find his comfort zone at the estate, as she realizes, Doug has never slept any place but the hauler, even at the ranch.

Amanda places the last of his clothes away, hears the water start, and the shower door shut.

"I'll be in the garden when you're ready to come down."

Amanda leans into the closed bedroom door with a remorseful sigh and bargains, "Oh Lord, oh Lord, what can I do to bring Doug's confidence back? I need to feel his strength and comfort."

She enters the garden, tells Alexa to play romantic music, and feels the peace only God can provide. Yes, there is no place closer to God than in a garden.

The wistful music heightens her anticipation. Amanda brushes the Callas and Hydrangeas. She chuckles as a bare spot appears she has so diligently scraped into existence. She gently shoos a grasshopper which Connie says loves to munch the Hosta's rich green leaves. Two white butterflies make a lazy circle while ascending. A hummer's slyness while in silent motion is soothing and spiritual. Amanda continues into the beautiful foray of lush greenness.

Doug, oh Doug, I have missed you, I just wish you felt more comfortable here. Amanda knows, that until a few weeks ago, the pleasures of a garden were unknown to her. Yes, this beautiful world of flowers. Amanda gently seats herself on the bench not knowing it was Charlie's peaceful spot as well.

Amanda turns with the shutting of the lanai door. Doug has two glasses. She flashes a smile, and rises as they tap drinks. She takes a sip. They begin to dance.

Their thoughts scatter to their other dance so long ago. Exhilaration, along with a state of euphoria, is unmistakable. They sway softly.

Yes, Doug's comfort and confidence return.

"Slow down."

"I know, I'm not speeding."

"No turn right at the next block and then park somewhere."

"That's not the attorney's office."

"I know but it is Wednesday!"

"You're mighty excited."

"Yup and you will be too. Wednesday's is Caramel Popcorn day."

JJ pulls to the curb and asks, "What is this?"

Connie glances to her right where JJ is nodding.

"Oh, that's El Reno City Hall, Water Department, and Council Chambers, but we're going there," and points to their left at the big red brick building.

"This is Ross Seed and Feed."

"So a feed and seed store has popcorn."

"Yes and much more."

JJ looks to the end of the building and the lot is filled with bedding plants. "Amanda wants some plants. Let's get some."

"That's sweet but she wants the opportunity to see, learn, and chose some flowers for herself."

JJ stops Connie from stepping forward so a car can pass.

"I can remember when looking both directions was not necessary but El Reno has come of age and come of age in a big way. They have not only hosted over thirty-four consecutive years of celebrating our famous fried onion burger at El Reno Burger Day but numerous spots air frequently on both TV and Radio stations proclaiming all the amenities available and always ends with, 'El Reno, close to you, far from ordinary'. I love it and I LOVE El Reno. My great grandmother told me stories of coming to town in a covered wagon and parking right here in the wagon yard as they shopped for goods to return to the farm. My Grandad owned a business a couple of streets over on Bickford. It was a poultry, feed, and supply company where people came and purchased a live chicken. Granddad would dress it and have it ready when they returned before they left town. I guess that's what they called a convenience."

"Why have you not told me all this?"

Connie turns somber, "Because the day we were here we unfortunately, had a difference of opinion and headed straight home even forgoing a hamburger."

JJ grabs her hand and nods his remembrance as they manage the car filled street and he says, "But not today. No, not today Connie."

After saying hello to Julie, Jennifer, and Teresa, Connie asks for two bags of caramel corn and turns to see JJ inspecting the kitchenware, food items, crosses, cow, pig, calf, and horse paintings, jewelry along with paint, tools, plumbing needs, electrical supplies and yes animal feed and garden seeds.

They munch away on the hot bags of sticky gooeyness as Connie says, "This is owned by the second and third generations and Walter Ross is still here quite often."

Connie glances at the clock. "We still have time for a quick drive before the firm closes. Let's go."

As they traverse the street Connie says, "Let's put the top down. What a glorious day for a ride on the strip. Turn left one block and then right onto Sunset Drive. I'm taking you west on HW 66 and yes, this is the famous Route 66 featured in many movies and TV shows."

They enter under the train trestle as Connie points out the murals. "Every viaduct and trestle all over town have paintings all depicting historic events involving El Reno."

"Yes, you showed me the one at MidFirst Bank, and what was that mural on the corner there?"

"Oh, Hero's Plaza remembering and celebrating our service men."

Here on the right, my great Aunt Carabell Casstevens lived during the forties. Turn here and I'll show you where my other Great Grandfather had the first cleaners in El Reno at the Southern Hotel. What a grand place it was. See he was right across from the train depot and the salesmen here conducting business would sit in a barrel while Grandpa pressed their suits."

JJ pulls to the curb and shoots Connie a look.

"True story. I've got pictures. It was right there."

JJ exits the car. "Can we go in?"

"We sure can. This is the Southern Hotel."

JJ stops after holding the door for Connie and looks at the original tile, columns, and marble steps leading up. They continue their tour, and nod at people sitting in the lobby as a whistle catches their attention."

"What's that?"

Connie rushes toward the door, "Hurry and we can see it," as the trolley comes into view.

Connie gleefully jumps up and down as she vigorously waves to the conductor and occupants who are eager to reciprocate.

"El Reno has the only rail-based trolley in Oklahoma. They had to excavate the tracks and the trolley had to be located and restored. All of this because of El Reno's wonderful visionaries with a love of history."

Connie glances at her watch as she tugs on JJ's arm, "Come on we have time for one more stop. El Reno is packed with not only one-of-a-kind features but tons of historical prospects that it will take more than the short time we have to not only cover, but digest everything El Reno has to offer."

In the car, they drive the short block to Sunset and head west.

"Where we going?"

"Just a couple of blocks and I want to stop and park. Here, turn in here. This is Jobe's Drive-In or use to be. My parents sat in their car night after night during the time they were dating and drank Cherry Vanilla Dr. Pepper, had Coke floats, and greeted all their friends who also were dragging the strip, burning gas, peeling out and I'm quite certain necking in a few corn fields, which I've been told was where Lake El Reno is now."

"You have a lake?"

"Aah J, another day, another day."

"Connie, you and your enthusiasm. I never thought I would love someplace so quickly."

"And you haven't even tasted a coney and burger yet."

FLAGG & FLAGG LAW FIRM

Upon entering the law firm, Connie and JJ are engaged in conversation about the Elk's Lodge to the north of the firm.

"It was purchased from the 1904 Louisiana Purchase Exposition and World's Fair held in St. Louis, disassembled, and brought here by train?"

"Yup. Very impressive. Is it open? Can we go in?"

"Not now but I might wangle an invitation." Connie offers with one eyebrow arched and a wink. "We can bring the kids."

"They don't do karaoke do they?"

They both laugh, give a high five and, fall into a partial hug as they remember the California outing to O'Brien's Irish Pub.

Connie feels JJ's embrace loosen. She turns and sees that they are being observed by clients exiting. She blushes, looks down, and moves quickly to the side.

"Mrs. Sinclair, please follow me to the conference room and I'll let Richard know you are here."

"Hey, guys. Good to see you again."

"You too. You're looking tan. Been to the lake?" Connie inquires.

"Yes, actually out at the golf course. Couldn't ignore this beautiful weather."

"I know. We had a drive through town with the top down. Just gorgeous."

Here are the documents you ask me to prepare. The only thing missing and this can be added after you sign Connie, is..." Richard turns his attention to JJ and continues, "Mr. Paige, I need your address."

JJ blinks, swallows and shifts slightly but it is Connie who confidently answers, "Mr. Paige's address is the same as mine. Then this conveys ownership of the OK Sportsman Club from me to Mr. Paige, including mineral rights, is that correct?"

"Yes, it is."

"Perfect."

"Connie, after you review, please initial the bottom of each page and sign the last page."

"Okay."

"While you're doing that, I will tell you the title is clear. I see no future problems other than the taxes haven't been paid. I can do that for you at the same time it's filed at the courthouse if you like."

"Thank you. So all further tax notifications will be received by mail?"

"Yes."

"Rosie, this is Connie."

"What's all the noise?"

"JJ and I are leaving El Reno and we have the top down. I'll make it quick."

"Oh, you ate onion burgers?"

"I wish, but no. Another time. Just wanted to tell you that we have met with the attorney and got the land transferred to JJ. He is officially an Oklahoma land owner, gives him a project and he will have to learn the back roads into town to cut down on the distance. He only knows the way coming 81."

"Well good luck with that one, JJ."

JJ answers, "I'm hoping GPS will help."

Connie asks, "You feeling okay? Sorry, I don't mean to holler!"

"Doing well. Anxious to see everyone."

"Me too, my friend."

"How are the wedding plans coming along?"

Connie chuckles. "Slow but sure."

"It will be wonderful. I can't wait. Still haven't gotten an invitation? I keep watching the mailbox."

"Yes ma'am. That's next on the list. They probably should have been out a month ago. Talk with you later. Love you."

"Love you too, Connie."

JJ reaches for her hand as Connie settles in, lays her head back and thanks God for all the pleasant moments she is being blessed with. *It's all you God, all you!"*

THE DANCE

No audible words are exchanged as they let this moment be a moment of complete surrender, yes, softly swaying to the music that melts away their weeks of separation. The separation and distance that allowed the feelings Amanda possesses and let, though small, so small, grow into feelings of fear of the future. Fear that should never be allowed to enter God's plan to prosper and not hurt, yet she had allowed these fears to grow and even empowered them to a point where she believed. Yes, she allowed them and believed them into being, a being of her rational reality where her fear of living with only Doug could not make a complete world.

Doug knows that he has made the right decision to return at the moment he has, even at the risk of a fall from the all-important standings for Magic and consequential loss of revenue for him and Connie. A fall from the needed continual rise through his show of strength at each successive race.

At this moment, none of that penetrates his thoughts. No, all that matters is where they have returned, yes, returned to when they were Doug and Amanda once again in California.

Doug strokes her arm tenderly with his index finger and whispers, "I love you so much that my heart aches every minute we are apart."

Amanda lends in closer, closer to the safety she desperately wants, needs, and desires to feel from him.

"You had me so worried last night. I heard what you said and the tone in your voice but not being with you to see your gestures and look into your eyes just unnerved me. I knew I had to come and come quickly. Can you understand that, Amanda?"

Amanda lays her head on his shoulder, and her breathing slows. The dance has ceased. It is just the two of them entwined as the music softly continues with two people so close that the beat of their hearts becomes one.

He pulls her back and stares into her eyes as if soul-searching.

She sees the tenderness he feels for her and believes it has never been so evident.

He knows he loves her more now than ever before. A smile tickles his lips. He kisses her as he has never kissed anyone. The feeling fills him as he continues to release the quivers from his stomach knowing they are being answered and replaced by her very being.

He looks at her and Amanda sees the deep want in his eyes. Amanda cries, wraps her arms around his neck, and knows the heartbeat of this man has countered her outcry that brought him ever so quickly to her side.

Doug has absorbed her insecurity as her need for safety and protection dissolves into oblivion. Yes, she can tell Doug!"

JEREMIAH JASON PAIGE

JJ pulls up the main entrance, and punches the button but the gates fail to open. JJ stares down the Sinclair insignia emblazoned on the gates and recognizes his mild irritation. The gates fail to open again. He punches the button repeatedly.

Connie notices his reddened face. "We can put the top up."

With the top up he would have used the unpaved north entry. Is Charles playing a game? What has brought this on?

He knew he was uncomfortable earlier when the matter of his address had been breached. What must the attorney think of him? Geri had called him Connie's 'gentlemen friend'. What should he care about the thoughts of other people? JJ assumed his growth in this area was becoming easier but is that a good thing? Either way, he will not dampen Connie's spirit today as she had told Rosie, 'there is a wedding to plan.'

He brings the car under the portico and successfully beats Connie to her door.

"Well thank you, kind sir," Connie babbles as she happily swings her legs from the car.

Before she can rise JJ leans in and runs his thumb from her cheek to her chin. Connie looks up, her eyes moisten momentarily as she once again looks into JJ's velvet brown eyes.

JJ thinks, *Can I do this? Is it time to advance further than friend status?*

Connie rises and after a shared hug, says, "I'll get the mail."

"No, I can. Besides I forgot the front door's entry code."

"Oh, that's easy, it's..." but Connie thinks better before continuing.

I guess it should be changed. It's Charles' and my anniversary.

Entering through the stained glass double doors onto marbled floors unexpectedly but pleasantly emits a calm coolness.

"You want the mail here or on the kitchen desk."

"Here's fine." She haphazardly sorts through as a line appears between her brows followed by, "I wonder?" She tosses the envelope aside and thinks another day.

JJ walks through the great room and says in a raised voice, "Hello, anyone home?"

"Maybe they are in the garden or perhaps the stable."

JJ hears the soft music as they walk out on the lanai. "Hum, abandoned drinks. A party?"

"If so it was a romantic one," Connie chuckles while displaying a slight crinkle on her nose.

JJ thinks, *Oh well, our romantic moments will have to wait.*

JJ feels a hollow spot breaching his stomach. "I'm getting hungry."

"Oh, shoot, if I had thought, I would have taken a container and brought coneys and burgers. Doug would have been grateful. There's always next time, I guess."

"If they aren't even here that wouldn't have worked." JJ snatches a hand full of grapes and says, "I'll ask Miguel."

"Okay, I'll grab something out of the freezer and get it in the oven," and then says, "Good ole Sams."

AMANDA BORDILLON

Oh, Lord, how can these few sweet steps shared between Doug and me, while lost in the quiet transforming music, have minimized my menacing thoughts and have moved me to this place of trust and contentment? Thank you, Lord isn't a garden the place You started this whole love thing Your love for us and our love for each other?. Yes, I can tell Doug!

Amanda takes a step back and with a smile of knowing entwines her fingers behind Doug's neck. "Doug?"

Doug, in a cloudy gaze, thoughts frozen, mind racing, searches for answers before he continues. "What, Amanda? What?"

"Can we talk?"

"Of course, always. If we don't talk situations can quickly be out of control."

Doug knows the preceding night he, himself was having difficulty making decisions. His fear of Amanda becoming detached from him was being recognized. He found he was obsessing over his possible flaws and shortcomings. Had he failed?

"Amanda, do you want to sit here?"

"No, let's walk." Amanda knows she needs a distraction as she can't say what she needs to while she looks at Doug."

"Could we go see Beauty?" *Yes, Beauty will give me courage.*

Doug opens the garden gate, places his arm around her, and draws her to his side. Doug steadies himself for one of two things, either full and unfettered resolution or reigning in his emotions on a damaged relationship and refocusing on solving the problem.

Beauty's stall is empty. Doug gives a whistle and the colt exuberantly trots forwards. They laugh.

Amanda rubs her colt. "You are growing too fast. I'm already looking up to you."

"You've missed him a lot and hopefully me also?"

"Oh, Doug, where do I begin?"

Doug, at this moment, braces for the uncertainty ahead.

"There is so much, so much I want you to understand. Doug, I have this fear that possesses me. I don't want to hurt anyone, disappoint anyone or make anyone sad."

Amanda goes silent as she lays her head on Beauty's neck and tears flow.

Doug ponders what to do. Do I console her or do I push her?

Doug pulls her from Beauty and just holds her as he feels the warmth of her tears on his neck.

"Amanda, we can't continue like this. I am useless to anyone when I don't know and can't understand my position, our position."

Amanda tells him about the fears of her heart. Is their love just a physical attraction and after the moment of release would their feelings change? Would the two of them alone be enough?"

"So what are you saying, you don't love me?"

"No, I know I love you! Since you are here I want nothing more than to never let you go."

Doug swallows back his need to shout gleefully as he feels his racing heart enfold Amanda's positive state of mind and acclamation of love even while being fearful.

"Then, that's all that matters, Amanda. You love me. The fear you are experiencing is the same I feel except my fear is never knowing what can be. We have these coming weeks before the wedding to acclimate our lives back."

Amanda stiffens at the mention of their wedding. He realizes her reluctance, unwillingness, and anxiety are a real aversion to marriage.

The tightening in his chest along with the tenseness in his muscles leaves him with the desire not to continue any further but he reluctantly presses on.

"You understand if the wedding is delayed it will have to be for a full year until the season's end next year!"

Doug knows he can't do this, not a year and his distress thrust him further. A longing to undo his sense of remorse engulfs him but he continues as he moves her back and lets his arms fall to his side. "Amanda, this is completely your decision. Is it now or do we wait?"

"Doug, oh Doug, yes, it's now but I can't tell them."

"Tell who? Tell what?"

"Connie and JJ. Connie is so excited and JJ has the surrey all refurbished but I quiver at the thought of this. It just keeps growing and growing and... I didn't realize it until I heard the plans, saw the surrey and they said Beauty would be with me, pulled behind, I wondered if he is ready for that if he is up to it and then I knew it was not only Beauty but I wondered if I could."

Amanda, with tears falling, raises her head, moves two steps back, looks intently into Doug's caring eyes, and sobs. "I know now I can't, I can't. Please, Doug, let's just go. You and I just leave, okay? We can be married on the way home. Just you and I."

A smile crosses Doug's face and quickly turns into a chuckle.

He draws his sad but oh-so-funny fiancé into his arms and laughs. "Yes, we can do that. An early wedding is no problem for me but with the three of us, that might be a problem."

"Yes, Magic also."

"No, you forgot about Miguel. Just the three of us on a leisurely drive across the country sharing our honeymoon! We will find another answer!"

"Hello, you all in here?"

"Yes, back here with Beauty, we'll be right there."

Doug gives Amanda a long hard hug that ends with an 'ump', a kiss to the forehead, and an offer of his hankie but too late as Amanda grabs her shirttail.

As they approach JJ and before JJ can ask the obvious 'what's wrong' question, Doug offers, "We were just going to take a trial run at pulling Beauty behind the surrey. Amanda is concerned he might not be willing to comply."

"Oh, okay, come when you're ready. I just wanted to tell you Connie has put dinner in the oven."

"You hungry, Amanda?"

"Yes."

Doug places his arm around her shoulder and they head to the house with Doug in a jovial mood, yes, now that he knows whatever the method, whatever the date and time, he would be married and all of that sooner than later.

CONSTANCE LOUISE SINCLAIR

"There you are. Hope everyone is hungry. Got salad, lasagna, and garlic knots."

"I'll set the table after I wash my hands. We've been loving on Magic and Beauty."

Doug jokes. "Well, more Beauty than Magic. Amanda, among other things, is afraid Beauty might not pull well behind the surrey."

Amanda places a plate, pushes her hair out of her face, and shoots a look at Doug but Doug's smile doesn't wain and he continues undaunted. Doug is a man with a mission, a mission to be married and finally be in control of his life. "Yes, Connie, we can talk later."

"What things, Amanda?" asks Connie, in a concerned tone as she pulls the casserole from the oven and says, "Not ready. Another twenty minutes". I know we are behind on the invitations, ordering the tents, and oh my, the guest list." She closes the oven and continues, "We will start first thing tomorrow. Doug, you write down everyone you plan on inviting. I don't think we have even determined a number. This might be a smaller event than Pete and Rosie's but it will be more intimate. You will be able to mingle. Yes, mingle and make everyone feel special and welcome."

Connie places her oven mitts on the counter and turns just in time to intercept a furtive glance between Amanda and Doug which quickly turns to a smile and nod.

"Okay, what's going on with you two?"

Amanda saves a spoon from precariously falling from the table and scurries off to retrieve the tea and glasses.

JJ helps place the glasses, pulls Amanda's chair for her, and says, "Sit down Sis. Let's talk."

Amanda sips her tea and looks at Doug.

JJ glances at Doug and continues, "It's obvious you two have come to some type of consensus so now it's time to include Connie and me. Who's going first?"

Doug begins, "Let's start with the only thing I wanted to hear and that is Amanda still wants to be married and to me!"

"That's wonderful so tomorrow we start and…"

JJ places his hand on Connie's arm as her words slow and then cease. He leans to catch Amanda's attention. "So is that correct? You and Connie start tomorrow with the grand plans?"

Amanda tries not to show her discomfort as self-consciously, with her head lowered begins. "Connie, I'm so sorry. I don't want to hurt you. I, I…" Amanda in a weakened voice stammers on, "I didn't realize that my fears weren't about Doug."

"Then what, Amanda?"

"It is the wedding or the big wedding. It wasn't until Doug was here and we are together that I knew I will follow him wherever live takes us but the wedding, the wedding…"

Connie stands. "Get up here. Give me a hug. You can't hurt my feelings. This is your day, well both of you."

Connie feels Charles' presence as tears begin to form. "This wedding is a minor detail and the important thing is that at the end of all this you are Mr. and Mrs. Douglas Hartly. Yes and tomorrow after you and Doug have made your decisions, J and I will be good listeners, but now, let's eat."

Right on cue, the timer is heard.

"Whew, saved by the bell."

"You finally going through that stack of mail? It's already hit the floor once so it's jumbled now."

"Yes, I kinda flip through it when I first get it, and if something looks pressing I'll open, if not, well this is the result." Connie sorts quickly. It is mostly junk mail because she has chosen to have everything sent electronically and all the estate utilities, insurance, etc. are paid through bank draft from her MidFirst household account.

The pile for the trash, she tosses on the floor then she sorts through the remainder and begins a stack for oil-related. There it is, the one she noticed when she and JJ entered through the front hall that is addressed to her through the trust account and from White Energy, LLC. She stands, and opens the envelope as this energy company is not one she has done business with.

The letter quickly announces Gene Rush is the land manager for White and is interested in leasing all or part of the section, township, and range she knows as OK Sportsman Club but of course all this before she signed everything to JJ.

"Here, this one is for you."

"Can't be, I've never done an address change from the ranch."

133

JJ takes the letter and says, "There's no physical address to this land, how do you know it's for me?"

"Get your packet that you got from the attorney. It should have copies of the documents he filed at the court house and the legal description should match that on this correspondence."

DOUGLAS HARTLY

The excitement Doug feels at continuing down the path to life with Amanda has finally hit him. He takes a little hop in the air as he exits the stables. He knows life will not always be smooth and untroubled, but he will do his best not to lead and also not to follow but just walk side by side, hand in hand with one foot in front of the other forever and ever.

He heads to the garden to find Amanda and continue the finalization of their wedding plans.

The last few days have been productive and he is anxious to tell Amanda that Miguel was still on board with transporting Magic back to California after he and Amanda leave on their honeymoon. Doug feels the need once again to hop in the air and maybe even add a little whoopee.

Amanda rises as she hears the gate and tosses her gloves and trowel in the basket used for clippings.

"Well, tell me. What did he say, was Miguel receptive?"

"No problem. I told him if he wanted I would fly José or Filipé here but he said he's good. I told him not to push it but navigation will be no problem as it is a straight shot on I40."

"So a week from Saturday will be our day. Oh, Doug, I would do it tomorrow but I can't deny Connie her flowers and JJ the surrey. Connie has ordered four hundred roses from Texas along with greenery and hydrangea."

"Wow, lots of flowers for our small wedding."

"I know, but she said she was okay with no big barbeque and dance band if I would indulge her on the flowers."

"And JJ feels the same way about the surrey. It will be perfect just us, the boys, Magic pulling you in the surrey and Beauty following."

"Have you heard back on the date change for the honeymoon? Yes, sorry, I should have told you the travel agency had no problem and we still have the same accommodations in Paris."

"No, I'm the one that's sorry. I know you wanted it all to be a surprise and then I walk in on you on the phone. I should have left and not told you I had heard but I was soooo surprised I just had to squeal."

"Amanda, don't ever do that. No secrets, no concealed feelings, no more unspoken truths no matter who it upsets."

"I know, I promise. Connie has made that quite clear. She says life is so short, we don't have time for hidden emotions and especially when we all love each other it is upsetting to not be informed and included."

DETECTIVE DANIEL DOBBINS

"Come in Pete. Got a lead on…"

"Danny, there has been another breach at the apartment. I've got to figure out a way to get Rosie and Chris gone without scaring Rosie."

"You thinking this is just an opportunist wanting in your apartment?"

"He has to be watching our place to know when we are gone. Either way, I'm not taking a chance."

"You've got Cleet training in a couple of weeks. You better cancel, or maybe not. Don't tell her you're not going."

"I've never lied to Rosie before."

"Do you even know of a safe location?"

"Yes, one."

CONSTANCE LOUISE SINCLAIR

"JJ, where are you?"

"Up here.

Connie climbs to the landing and stops as JJ leaves his bedroom and notices the big smile on her face.

"What's so funny?"

"Just laughing at how awkward our sleeping arrangements are."

"How so? You inviting me into your enter sanctum?"

"You wish!" Connie says as she pokes JJ. "No, Doug is on the other side of me and Amanda is in between both of us."

"Well, at least you and Doug aren't sharing the same bath. Let's just say there is a lot of door knocking going on and then half the time I have to walk around as the door from the bath to my bedroom is locked because she forgets."

"What did you decide on the bank? You moving everything to El Reno and did you call White Oil?"

"I'm going to open an account here and decide on closing my California account later," says JJ.

"And the oil lease through White?"

"Haven't called yet."

"I was anxious to know. Leases can bring in a nice income. If it has been leased already Flagg's would have caught it."

"Let's go down. You want a coffee or should I say you want 'fancy' coffee?"

"Give me a break. I only do fancy coffee in the afternoon."

JJ hits the button on the Keurig, turns, and places his arms around her. "Less than a week and the kids will be out of here. You're missing all the pageantry of a big wedding aren't you?"

"I thought I would, but not really."

JJ hands Connie her cup and as she places the caramel syrup and cream in, she says, "I think everything worked out for the best, but…"

"But what?"

"I was just thinking all the money the wedding would have cost maybe we give them some money for their honeymoon. They could buy something, yes, they could buy something special as a memento of their Paris trip."

"That would be nice."

Connie says, "What time is it?"

"Too late for the bank if that's what you're thinking."

"But not too late to go to Charles' office. I want to get everything out of his office safe anyway and don't want to do it with a group of people around. I know there is cash there."

"How much are you going to give them?"

Connie suddenly realizes she has not included JJ in the gift-giving and tries to craftily continue. "You know when we talked before Amanda arrived that we are going to gift them with the balance of shares to Magic. They will be sole owners and that's as it should be. Amanda loves Magic and Magic loves her. She was there from the moment he was unloaded at the ranch and I know she filled a void because I was usually there for him."

JJ places his coffee on the bar and takes a seat.

Connie continues, "You do remember, don't you?"

"Yes, I'm good with that. I bought half ownership to Magic from Doug but if you are doing cash also I want to do half or match whatever you are thinking."

Connie thinks, *Thank you, Lord for getting me out of that situation.*

"Okay, a couple of thousand. You a thousand and me a thousand?"

"Yup," chuckles JJ.

"What's so funny?"

"You'll have to float me a loan! You do take checks, don't you?"

PREP DAY

The flowers are delivered and the task at hand is to get them immediately in tubs of water. The roses have to have the thorns and outside petals removed. Amanda picks the flowers for her bouquet and Connie's friend, Vickie, who does all of the weddings, wraps the stems in satin and secures them with pearl top pins. A smaller bouquet is fashioned for Connie as maid of honor and boutonnieres are made for Doug and his best man, Michael even Magic and Beauty are to have flowers on their bridles.

The kids opt for a morning wedding and decide to have a small luncheon of curried chicken salad on soft buttery croissants with a mandarin, kiwi, avocado tossed fruit platter. Oh, but the cake. The most time was spent on the cake. Doug doesn't want a groom's cake even after being told it could be double fudge and topped with chocolate-covered strawberries.

Amanda's favorite is white and suddenly Doug's is white, also. Doug assures Connie that he is good with whatever makes Amanda happy. After considerable prodding, Doug admits he is more of a pie guy and pecan on top of that.

JJ is staying neutral and finds busy work alongside Vickie.

Connie and Amanda visit two of the best bridal couture in Oklahoma City, and Amanda's dress is perfect; white satin, short sleeve, barely off the shoulder with sequin and pearls at the waistline to accentuate Amanda's tiny waist. Amanda choses a sheer veil attached to a petite tiara and the finishing touch was to be her mother's opal necklace but it had gotten crushed in her purse on the way to Oklahoma. Amanda is heartsick because she had no idea how fragile the necklace was.

The dining room is adorned with a plethora of bouquets and seating for all attendees is easily handled even with the addition of Pete and Rosie the grand total of fifteen seems an understatement to the elaborate preparations.

Tables are placed in each of the far corners of the dining room. The first table is smaller but stands higher and holds two pictures. One of Amanda's mother Margaret and the other of Charles but Connie knows it isn't Charles because Amanda has chosen a picture of Charlie, as she knew him in jeans, a plaid shirt, and leaning against a rail fence. The sign in front of the vase of flowers between the frames states simply, 'Wish you were here!'

The second table holds the cake on a crystal circle elevated on cut-crystal orb feet with flowers extending from beneath, upward, and around each of the three layers. Connie has asked for three layers so the top can be frozen and resurrected on Doug and Amanda's first anniversary. The guys think resurrected is the appropriate word and all laugh.

Everyone needs to hang on for in less than twenty-four hours the small wedding is to become...

THE BIG EVENT

JJ wakes early but he quickly finds the bathroom off limits as Connie opens the door to his knock and forces his shaver, toothbrush, toothpaste, and deodorant in his arms and finishes with a kiss on her finger and plants it on the end of his nose.

JJ wanders to the hall and looks waywardly toward Doug's room, shakes his head, and dejectedly descends the stairs to the laundry bathroom. He enters the kitchen where he is met with 'good mornings' from several people he has never laid eyes on.

Exasperation overtakes him. He backs several steps and turns to hear Connie say, "Babe, not there. Use my bath."

No one had told him he will need written instructions and technical training to make it through this day. He makes it to the base of the stairs where his juggling act between his toothpaste and deodorant ends with his deodorant the looser as it tumbles to the floor where the plastic container separates on contact with the marble.

He bends but is standing on the leg of his pajama pants which yanks them below his hips. He throws the additional encumbering items in his arms on the stairs and grabs his wayward pants as he hears, "Oops, sorry for the intrusion. I'll let you get pulled together and then we can talk."

JJ whirls around to see Vickie turning her back in his direction. He straightens his pants and tucks his tee shirt and bemoans, "Okay, I'm good. What can I help you with?"

"I need access to the surrey and bridles the ponies will be wearing."

"I'll call Miguel and he can meet you at the north end of the stables."

JJ fumbles in his pockets before he realizes he has no phone.

"I'll call from upstairs. Give me five minutes."

"Thank you."

JJ waits as she exits the room but still checks the area before he bends to retrieve his items and wipes the gel deodorant from the floor with his pant leg.

Showered and dressed he stops and knocks on Doug's door with no answer as Connie opens the bathroom door and says, "Babe, Doug is getting dressed in the RV," and quickly shuts the door before he can reply.

JJ looks at the base of the stairs for deodorant residue, and advances a couple of steps before being met by a girl with a box of flowers and says, "Your name is?"

"JJ."

She fumbles through each tag and exclaims, "Here you are. Could I put this on for you?"

JJ places his hands on his hips, and feels his impatience growing but musters a smile.

The fiddling continues until she scornfully says, "Let me get Vickie, this is crooked."

The moment she disappears JJ makes a speedy exit through the sunroom and a bee-line for the RV only to stop and exclaim, "Where the...where did the hauler go?"

JJ stands with legs apart as he rubs the back of his neck and Miguel points to the east side of the stables.

Doug opens the door at the first knock and JJ staggers to the couch.

"JJ you okay? What's going on? Something happen inside?"

"Yeah. Let me catch my breath. Man, it's a mad house in there. It's like I woke up in a different place."

Doug smiles and lets out a hardy laugh. "So Connie found you, too!"

JJ exhales a 'whew' and notices Doug's calm demeanor.

"I'm in there fighting for my life and you're out here kicked back watching TV. Some friend you are. Where's Mike?"

"He's with Magic and bringing Amanda in the surrey."

"Won't be long now!"

****

"Amanda, Amanda, oh Amanda, you are beautiful. Doug will be speechless," exclaims Connie.

"That's okay as long as he can say, I do."

"Bet there is no problem there. Let's go, Vickie said they are ready for pictures with you, Magic and Beauty."

Connie kisses her cheek and says, "I'm going to take my seat. See you in a few."

"Oh Connie…Connie, thank you."

****

The surrey bells are heard in the distance. The fundamental purpose of the day has begun. Attendees rise in anticipation of the moment. Magic is held to a slow trot while the little guy bounces awkwardly to the side.

The morning sun is to their back and the glistening rays dance on every facet of the procession.

One guest comments, "Precious, just precious."

JJ helps Amanda down. They walk the short distance and make the turn toward Doug. Doug takes a step forward knowing that his capacity to love has been underestimated.

Connie savors this fleeting sliver of time, glad to be alive, and thanks God for all the good things in life but suddenly thinks, *Something's missing. Have I just been too busy…no Charles, I haven't felt you. Charles, where are you? Just then Charles comes and Connie thinks, you can't leave me.*

The minister asks, "Who gives this bride to be wed?"

JJ answers, "Her family and I."

Doug accepts Amanda's hand and turns toward her. He slowly raises her veil and their eyes lock. The minister continues about promises being made not only to each other but to God as the birds sing softly their song of two people's love, only through God, transformed into one.

The kiss is outstanding as Doug dips her back and finishes with a flurry and twirl toward the guests.

The minister officially says, "It is my great honor to present to you Douglas and Amanda Hartly.

Everyone walks to the surrey as they cheer the couple on. Magic prances away as the couple kiss once more.

Connie scurries off to escort the guests through the gardens onto the lanai and through the sunroom. Vickie and her team move the mountains of flowers from the surrey to the reception area.

Wine and cocktails are served to the guests as they mingle and comment.

Rosie finds Connie, hugs her, and says, "Well done. This is beautiful."

Pete adds, "Very nice. Where has the time gone, didn't we just get married here a couple of months ago."

Connie agrees, "Yes you did."

The kids enter and Mike offers in a chiding fashion, "The bride and groom have entered the building. Let the festivities begin!"

Connie urges, "Yes, please everyone find your seat."

JJ holds Connie's chair and she confides, "I think it is a success."

JJ chuckles and nods in Mike's direction as Mike eyes the chicken salad. JJ explains, "I think he was hoping for ribeye."

"Too early in the day for steak."

"Utt oh, Pete might beg to differ with you on that too."

"Shh! They will hear you."

Before the cake is cut, Mike stands and asserts, "Please join me in a toast to the couple." Mike exhales and continues, "Doug and Amanda, may your journey through life be at a slow and leisurely pace because you are both winners in this race!"

The clinking of glasses is heard as the toast is greeted with agreements of, "Here, here!"

"Connie, could we talk somewhere?"

"Where's Rosie?"

"The bathroom. That's why I wanted to take this opportunity to ask you something."

"Give me that baby. Come here, Christopher."

"You got him?"

"Yes. What is it, Pete?"

"I've got a problem, it's about Rosie and Chris. I have to be out of town. They tapped me to be at a CLEET seminar and Rosie and the baby have a doctor's appointment. I always go when they both are getting shots."

"I can take her. I'll be glad to because our girl time has been few and far in between."

"That will be great. Chris will be fine but someone needs to be with Rosie for the first forty-eight hours after her injection."

"Rosie and I can work that out. Your place or ours. Wherever she feels comfortable."

"No, not our apartment."

Connie gives Pete an incredulous stare. "Okay."

Pete thinks, *Now can I get Rosie to believe this is necessary?*

AMANDA BORDILLON HARTLY

"Douglas Christian Hartly, you get over here, you're helping with this. These are to both of us. See, Doug and Amanda Hartly! Makes my heart flutter, Doug and Amanda Hartly."

"Ohh," swoons Mike, "Douglas Christian!"

Doug had seen the two adorned high-back chairs but was still hanging on to the swiftly diminishing hope that Connie would occupy one of the seats.

"Let's start with that big one."

Doug positions the gift between their seats and pulls the wrapping from his side as Amanda swiftly makes short work of hers. Doug stands and lifts the tall sculpture positioning it lengthwise. Everyone makes approving resonances as they realize it is Hartly sculpted from horseshoes.

Mike quickly takes credit as several congratulate him for his endeavor.

The cards contain cash with notes to purchase something significant on their honeymoon in Paris. Several had gift cards to restaurants with memos saying, 'Special Occasion Dates'.

After the last gift had vanished and the happy couple stood to thank everyone, JJ steps forward and says, "Wait, not so fast. Here is one more from Connie and me."

Doug sees the back of a frame and wonders what the photo could be.

JJ turns the picture and confides proudly, "As you know, I purchased half interest in Magic a few years ago and gifted it to Connie and now it is gifted from us to each of you with our best wishes on your wedding day."

Mummers were heard throughout the room, especially from Doug's racing buddies.

Doug lowers his head as he is humbled and Amanda's eyes glisten.

Charles' effervescence is felt by Connie and she rubs her arms to enhance his presence.

Doug and JJ exchange handshakes but not the girls, no it's hugs and lots of them.

Everyone claps and then Doug raises his hands to quiet the room. "Could I have your attention? Thank you."

Doug looks at Amanda and pulls her to his side and questions, "You or me?"

"You do it."

Doug clears his throat and continues, "We want to thank everyone for sharing our day, blessing us with your presence and your generosity. We are beyond words." Doug smiles at Amanda and kisses her on her forehead.

"As you are aware the ranch in California has ponies and lots of them from the Bureau of Land Management. When JJ made the arrangements and the Mustangs were transported to their new home we had several mares with foal and one of the first to be born was...well, you saw him tethered to the surrey earlier. Amanda named him Black Beauty as he is Magic's twin in every way."

Doug stammers and looks to the floor, "I guess what I'm trying to say is...Connie and JJ, Amanda and I want you to have Black Beauty to keep here at the estate. We know he can't replace Magic but Amanda seems certain that through some divine power he was born Magic's double."

Connie shivers as she welcomes Charles once more.

ROSIE REDMOND ROSEMAN

"Connie, Pete told me his arrangement for us."

"You're not upset?"

Rosie after a minor huff, says, "Yes, at first, but Pete seems to think it necessary for someone to be present since Chris and I both are having shots."

"And side effects."

"Yes, the doctor said there is a possibility of side effects so, I will welcome your presence just in case I need help with Chris, and besides it's been a while."

"I know, that's exactly what I told Pete but what I didn't tell him was about the shopping spree."

"Good thing you didn't or he might have rethought the whole arrangement. You know men, always taking care of their women."

If only she knew.

CONSTANCE LOUISE SINCLAIR

Connie awakes, ready to greet another day. She pulls on shorts and a top before descending the staircase. Connie halts after a few steps as she notices the stillness of the moment. The quiet invades her space as if mocking her every movement. How long will it take her to not miss Amanda's voice filled with the delightful observation of everyday life? Yes, this will be challenging.

Connie enters the kitchen and looks in both directions as she says, "J, are you…" Her words hang in the air as she hears Magic's whinny of resistance.

Connie races to the door flings it open, and advances shoeless toward the stables. Magic battles against Miguel's repeated efforts to move him toward the hauler. Connie grabs the reins and in an attempt to calm her horse softly says, "Magic, it's okay, Magic, calm down," but Magic bolts and drags Connie before she loses her grip and is thrown clear as Magic resists being placated and bolts toward the north entrance gate.

JJ jumps from the hauler ramp with his hat in hand and turns Magic. Miguel grasps the lead and runs beside the horse until he gets Magic to a stop at the portico entrance.

Connie reaches Magic, strokes his neck, and talks gently while Magic dances rhythmically in place. She turns him back into himself then in a large oval as she moves him nearer to the portico then the hauler. The moment their course is in line with the ramp Magic voices his displeasure, lifting his front hoofs from the ground.

On the final turn, Miguel meets them with a bucket of oats and taking great care leads the stallion forward to his stall.

Connie looks down at the abrasions on her legs and says to JJ, "Of all days to have shorts on."

Connie feels Charles' presence and strokes her arms in recognition. *What are you saying, Charles? I don't understand.*

"Yup, what a way to start the morning," JJ agrees as he dusts the legs of his pants with his hat.

Connie walks toward the portico and turns. "Poor baby. I feel…"

"No," JJ interrupts, "I should have asked you. I knew it was a bad sign when Magic backed to the end of his stall to avoid Miguel. Maybe if you had been out here."

Miguel comes to Connie and JJ. "He is settled now. What do you wish me to do?"

"Give us some time to think this through."

JJ and Connie enter the house. "Do you think it's because Doug and Amanda aren't present?"

"No." Connie immediately feels Charles' presence and stammers, "No, I think he knows this is home. You could see it the minute Magic exited the hauler that first day but this still makes no sense. Magic gets transported to races all the time."

"Well if the races are to happen," JJ continues, "Magic and Miguel need to be on the road no later than tomorrow. Doug has lost a large amount of money after the Ruidoso forfeiture and not to mention the loss in standings.

JJ accepts a glass of water from Connie and after emptying the glass says, "I think I should go along."

Connie stands, "If you're going, I am too. I'll call the Wilsons. Let's start packing and we can get some miles behind us before dark."

JJ says, "I don't need much. You go pack and I'll settle Magic some more."

"Miguel, we're all going to make the trip. We can't take a chance of Magic bolting on you somewhere on the road. Get Magic and walk him around the hauler several times."

JJ enters the back door and finds Connie sitting at the desk with the uplifted phone and her hand over her mouth.

"Did you call the Wilsons?"

"I started to but then I remembered I can't go."

"Why?"

"I promised Pete I'd be with Rosie. Pete is leaving and I have been entrusted to be with her in case she has a reaction to her next shot and to help with Christopher."

"This can't wait, Connie. Magic has to be at the ranch and rested before Doug and Amanda's return. I'll go."

Connie feels Charles once again. *What Charles, what?*

Connie stands, walks to the sink, leans back, and states, "I don't want you to go and I can't go but I have trepidations about you going without me. Oh JJ, you have to stay."

JJ advances as he realizes Connie's need to be held. "It's okay, I'll get José or Filipe on a plane immediately."

ROSIE REDMOND ROSEMAN

"Connie, are you on your way to get me?"

"Yes, I am. Get your and Chris' shots out of the way and we can have some R & R at the estate. JJ and I need to stick close. Miguel and José left yesterday with Magic for the ranch. JJ was insistent they call periodically. Magic was acting all flighty and we couldn't take a chance on him possibly bolting and getting hurt. JJ wanted to go but, Rosie, I felt Charles and begged JJ to stay."

"*Well, well, Charles*. Sounds like a good reason to me."

"JJ immediately said he would fly José here. So JJ will be at his…land. Boy, I need to figure out a name so JJ can have some semblance of ownership instead of calling it the OK Sportsman Club.

Otherwise, the only thing we've got is a couple of interviews for stable hands and one is promising as he and his wife live between the estate and Piedmont."

"Did you get more ponies?"

"Not yet, but it is being considered, though for now, we need someone to continue with the gentling of Black Beauty."

"That's okay. I've only packed lounging clothes mostly."

"And your bathing suit?"

"Nope, I didn't."

"No problem, I've got plenty. Rosie, you're not feeling well?"

"I'm okay, I just feel punk."

"Punk? Is that like in a funk?"

"Yeah, I guess I'm in a funk, I'm feeling a little uneasy about the DA possibly dropping the charges on weird guy."

"No, no. It's all done with the transfer from me to JJ, or that is my attorney's inclination. Now we can focus on what Charles has underway. Are you up for some amateur sleuthing? It will be a challenge for both of us. Keep our minds busy."

DRISCOLL AND DRISCOLL LAW FIRM
MATTHEW DRISCOLL

"What are you doing here? Did anyone see you? Where's Arthur?"

Matthew gives Kirby a look and points to a chair. Matthew locks his main entrance and side entrance he uses to leave without being seen, and hits a button while he walks to look out on the parking lot.

"Julie, is Arthur available?"

"I'll ask."

Matthew glares at Kirby, he is furious.

"No, he's out the rest of the day and if you don't need me, I'm leaving also. I have a couple of papers for you to review and I'll…"

"Leave them for tomorrow. Good evening."

Matthew motions Kirby to silence until he is certain Julie has left. Matthew walks to the window to be certain Arthur's parking spot is vacant.

Kirby stands and paces.

Matthew becomes further annoyed.

"You know those two girls we had at the cabin. Keri and her friend…"

JEREMIAH JASON PAIGE

"That was Miguel and they are only able to do four hours or so a day. He said the heat while crossing the desert is going to be miserable. He is concerned about Magic's stamina even with the air-conditioned hauler."

"That's not good. I was hoping for quick and easy, especially since Magic was in such a state."

"Connie, maybe I should have made the trip."

"Magic seemed okay after José got here. I know Miguel, José and Felipe have been with Magic enough to at least partly stabilize him and his excess energy. After all, he is used to training and hasn't had any runs to amount to much being here."

"I hope so," states Connie. *Oh, Charles, I hope you're right about not letting JJ go."*

CONSTANCE LOUISE SINCLAIR

"Rosie?"

"In here, in the Sunroom."

"Oh, I'm being so loud and you have him asleep. Do we need to get a rocker in here? We're not used to being quiet."

"No rocker for him and you don't have to be worried about being quiet either. When Chris is tired he just wants to be laid down and he's out. I can move his bed and run the sweeper right under him and around him. He never wakes up."

"Connie chuckles walks to her friend, and squeezes her on the shoulder. Glad you're feeling better. You are aren't you?"

"Yes, I'm feeling more secure and it's all thanks to you Connie you always keep my heart light."

"Aww, that's sweet. Are you hungry? Do you want to have lunch on the lanai? Do you know what you want?"

"Whatever you and JJ are having is fine."

"Just us, J is at the…the…place. What are we gonna call it? Never mind, you know. So outside or in?"

"Out. I never get to be out at the apartment, but what about the flies and besides Connie, it looks like rain."

"It will be lovely on the lanai even during a rain and the flies wouldn't dare bother us as we have Martins. The Martins will stay until the end of July and then it will be a free-for-all between the flies and the mosquitoes. Come I'll show you!"

Connie returns from the kitchen with the loaded tray and joins Rosie.

"Listen, the birds. You can already hear them before we open the doors. Here the chatter, that's them. Wait let me help you lift his bed over the threshold. Glad this is on rollers. Sweet baby, he smiles while he sleeps."

"The internet says that that's probably gas."

"Do tell."

Connie grabs a couple of pairs of sunglasses from their basket and offers, "Here, take a pair."

"You and your sunglasses. You never can find them in your purse and it's no wonder as they are all in this basket."

Connie walks through the French doors while inhaling the smell of eminent rain and points to the area high on the mountings holding the Martin houses.

"Let's walk out so you can see them in flight. They are aerodynamic and soar to the heavens. They land but usually only at their apartments."

"Do they come to the bird feeders?"

"No, never. We have seen them on the ground, well, Charles and I at least, it was after a hurricane hit south Texas and the tropical depression sat on top of us and dropped rain for days; the martins would land at the edge of the resulting ponds to catch the insects.

That's when Charles planted that Golden Wisconsin Willow because he knew exactly where water would pool and willows love water. Now look at it, it must be over ten years old."

"It's beautiful and the breeze just helps to make its foliage glimmer in the sun," says Rosie wistfully.

"Yes, and it makes a nice wind break also."

Connie notices Rosie's melancholy voice just as the rain begins. "Let's eat. Cranberry chicken salad and it even has purple grapes."

No answer from Rosie but her demur state of mind is evident.

"Let me look at your injection site. What did the doctor tell me to look for?"

Connie is fully aware of the doctor's orders but wants to facilitate further conversation.

"You're to make certain there is no change in color or red streaks."

"Good, nothing so far."

Rosie seems content to offer minimal answers.

Connie takes another bite, lifts her napkin, blots her mouth, and leans back in the porch rocker.

Rosie continues with her last bite.

Connie rocks forward. "You want to talk?"

"I thought that was what we're doing."

"No," charges Connie. "I'm talking and talking to the point I'm having to cajole you into joining the discussion. When I have you engaged in conversation you are upbeat and affable but the minute there is a lull in our conversation you revert to your thinking mode. I KNOW you're thinking mode. See, you haven't even noticed the rain."

Rosie exhales, pushes her rocker back, and pulls her legs under her. "I'm okay. I have these moments, these moments when it's the little things, like a sunset, the warmth of running water on my hands, and even the sound of your chattering birds that brings me to a place where I start to contemplate the significance of everything. It's the simplicity of life, yes the simple things like Chris someday playing in this sweet summer rain. Connie, I can so easily let my head be turned to the terror I felt when the doctor told us what a high-risk pregnancy we would experience and no guarantees to the outcome."

Connie is at Rosie's side.

"And our moments in the cellar."

Their hands each cup the others, as their bond through so many perils is tearfully remembered.

"Oh Rosie, it's almost too much when memories are connected to the physical moment in which you find yourself."

SINCLAIR STABLES

Connie sees Beauty in Magic's stall and is struck by the small stature of her colt. Beauty whinnies trots to the gate, and stops. Connie places his grain in the trough, and strokes him. Her eyes stare to the pasture beyond to memories best left unvisited.

"Connie, it's going to take a lot of oats for Beauty to fill Magic's place but he can do it. He still has a lot of growing to do."

A gentle smile returns to Connie's face. "Yes, it will take some growing but I have confidence in you little guy. First, though, we have to decide what you want to do when you grow up. Do you want to run, or maybe you would rather be a cutting horse or a cross country jumper, or even better let's get you into reining. I love reining horses. JJ is working with Doug about your future."

"Reining?"

"Yes ma'am, the NRHA Derby is in Oklahoma City next week and we are going. It's the last stop before Vegas and the Run for a Million. It's the top reining show and Doug thinks reining is where Beauty is showing stability."

"NRA what??"

"Not NRA, that's guns, NRHA, National Reining Horse Association."

"Great. I'm always interested in new adventures."

"We have been invited by Dave and Vickie, the lady that does all our weddings. She has a cousin's daughter, Calla that will compete. She's only been in the saddle for a year but has taken to it, well, like a duck, you know."

Beauty has stopped eating as if to listen.

Connie smiles, "You eat now and there will be time to decide your future later."

"May I pat him?"

"Yes. Give me Chris. Come here, sweet baby."

Rosie rubs between his ears as the colt is undisturbed by her touch.

"Rosie, stroke his shoulders right behind his mane, that's where his mother nuzzles him to settle him when he's anxious."

"He is so soft and more my size. Magic is so immense and he does that little prancy thing. I never know where to stand."

"Yes, I can see where you would feel that way."

"Connie, I believe that Beauty will be a great comfort to you and I think Amanda was wise in recognizing the loss you feel with Magic permanently in California. I agree with Doug."

"About what."

"At their wedding he said Amanda thinks, through some divine power, Beauty was born Magic's double."

"Yes, he did," mumbles Connie, and then, "Okay Lord, I can hardly wait to see where you take this baby."

Charles is present. Connie rubs her arms.

"Connie, I've been anxiously awaiting your call!"

Connie's silence exacerbates Geri.

"Connie, I wanted to do this in person but time is running out. Do you have time to speak now?"

"Yes, Geri, I'm so sorry. I'll be right up."

"No, Ben is at the barn, but can pop in at any moment, so please indulge me."

"Okay."

"We have been notified and it has been confirmed, that Jake is going to be released on parole."

"Oh Geri, you had me worried as I was under the impression this was something complicated. You should be ecstatic."

"I am but that brings me to our previous conversation. I need your help. One of the requirements for Jake's early release is a job, and he has only two months to produce pay stubs for his probation officer. You know there would be no qualms with him working here at the dairy and that is what Ben is determined he does.

"Seems logical."

"No, that is not what Jake wants. I'm trying to be the peacemaker and run interference. Jake needs a job and I was hoping you might have a position. Connie, if you could find it in your heart to employ him, I will pay every penny of Jake's wages. I know I am asking a lot, but Connie…"

"Geri, say no more. You do believe in God's divine providence in our lives don't you?"

"Well yes. So are you saying you will do this?"

"That's exactly what I'm saying. I have acquired, as a gift, a sweet pony with more on the way and I AM in need of a stable hand or two. See, God has answered Jake's prayer and at the same time fills my need. It's a win, win!"

"Rosie, where are you?"

"In here."

"I'm done with the stable hand and it worked out wonderfully. Yes, better than I ever thought, but…"

"Yes."

"Yes, but before he got here, I spoke with Geri, you know north of us?"

"Geri?"

"You remember Geri and Ben Wilson?"

"No…a??"

"Yes you do, Geri and Ben the section north. They were supposed to watch the estate when I went to California. Doug had called and was concerned about Amanda as she was trying to adjust to the realization that Charles was her father?"

"Okay, we went up there, and had coffee but there was a family problem?"

"Right. Jake, their oldest, was in trouble and facing incarceration and that's what's so wonderful. He is being paroled and needs a job. Jake told Geri he wants to work here. That is what Geri has been trying to get ahold of me about. Jake wanted her to call and see if I possibly had something for him."

"He did, did he?"

"So Jake and Mike Dixon will share duties. Isn't that wonderful we get a stable hand and Jake gets his job!"

"Yes, he does."

Rosie's mind jumps in a dozen directions but foremost she knows what Pete's first reaction will be and not only that, she knows what his second, third and fourth response will be and that's after he calms down.

"See everything is settling down, finally. The kids are married, Magic will be back on the circuit and we have someone for Black Beauty while helping out our neighbors. Nothing to worry about."

Rosie walks to the north window, looks toward the Wilsons, and thinks, *yup, nothing at all.*

Connie methodically turns.

"Although, maybe Mike Dixon isn't the right guy to place with Jake."

"Because…"

"I don't want to do anything to put Jake in a confrontational position."

"Over what?"

"It was just something that he mentioned when I was interviewing him. I told him Jake was being released, and he would be backing Jake up when he had to meet with his parole officer."

"What did he say?"

Connie stands and walks to the French doors leading to the balcony. "He mentioned he was aware of the Wilson boy's problem and felt sorry for anyone who found his girl with that guy. He said he knows him and he's no good, and Jake doesn't need to tangle with him because it wouldn't turn out well."

"What do you think?"

"Jake walks in and finds, Keri, his girlfriend, in bed with another man, and wasn't there something else?"

JEREMIAH JASON PAIGE

"Hey ladies."

Connie rises as JJ brushes her cheek with a kiss. "We didn't hear you come in. You hungry?"

"No, but thanks. I'm home early. The rain has the arena flooded and the construction crew left."

Rosie nods toward his feet. "I can tell no boots they must be outside."

"I'm headed to the shower," JJ states as he exits but then turns and walks back. "Oh, I talked to the Landman from White Oil and I think you will find this interesting. He said he had been trying to get the oil lease on this property for years and was surprised when I returned his call."

JIM NORICK ARENA
OKLAHOMA STATE FAIRGROUNDS

"Rosie, sit here because any information you get will be more beneficial coming from Dave and Vickie. These two have been in the horse business for years and if there's something one of them won't know the other will."

Dave leans in. "You all can see the signs posted around the arena. But front and center are Yellowstone, 1883, Paramount's precursor to Yellowstone, and Four Sixes Ranch signs. Out of those three, the Four Sixes is the only one truly in existence."

"Dave, we forgot to tell you. After you let us out we were headed to see an acclaimed stud that's new at one of the large ranches, and Vickie spotted a film crew in Barn 1. All the lookers were there and Vickie told me and Rosie to get our picture with the dark beard guy, sunglasses, and hat. Yup, it was him, but not one of us had our phones. You had them all in our purses in the SUV."

"Yeah, they are shooting part of their show here. You remember last season the ranch owner decided to spend mega bucks to get him into the horse business and pull a team together for him? Bet they are doing their horse shopping here. It must be nice to have all that imaginary money funding your purchases."

"When does the season begin?"

"Beat's me. Look the first finalist is entering the ring. The announcer is giving you all the information on the rider and horse but look at the monitor. See the horse's name and underneath the sire and dam. The largest part of the big winners will either be from a Gunner sire/dam, a Whiz sire/dam, or even O'Lena. Ima Doc O'Lena was a great stallion consistently in the top ten standings. In the late nineties, he was inducted into the Appaloosa Hall of Fame and has ties to El Reno. Watch the screen as there is a Lena pedigree in the finalist category. All in all, every horse's pedigree more than likely can be traced to King Ranch in Texas. The ranch dates back to 1853 and is often called the birthplace of racing."

"One of our friends, Robin and her mother, began forty years ago cataloging all the pedigrees and their business was so successful that AQHA purchased the company."

"Hello sweetheart, how's it going? The baby okay?" Did you two get your shots?

"Yes, but Chris put up a howl."

"Oh no."

"Pete, it broke my heart. I guess I wasn't holding him right because he didn't cry when you were there. What did you do that I didn't?"

"I rubbed his back and neck to see if I could get his attention off the injection."

"Well, I was clueless."

"You two have any side effects?"

"No, thank you, Lord."

"That's just great. You know I miss you!"

"I miss you too, Pete."

"Oh, remind me to increase my life insurance."

"What, why?"

"Because that is what responsible people do when they have a family."

CONSTANCE LOUISE SINCLAIR

"Connie walks into the gallery and plops in the armchair. You didn't write on the notepad on the bar. You remember you were the one that suggested we use it instead of walking and yelling."

"I'm sorry. I did make that suggestion. I came in here to talk to Pete. I think this is my favorite place, especially in the afternoons when Chris is all settled."

"I know, he is such a good baby."

"Will we see JJ tonight? I missed him last night and this morning."

"I can call and see what his schedule is like. He's all caught up in the new place or should I say the ranch."

"You have a name?"

"Yes, J just happened to say it on a call to a contractor. He said, 'Have it delivered to the ranch on Hefner Road'. He is erecting a metal barn with custom stables, buildings for offices, and a large covered arena. There is a lodge made from roughhewn timbers that he says is pretty spectacular and is anxious to start renovations after the arena and offices are complete. Doug is coaching JJ via Skype as Black Beauty seems to have the temperament to become a cutting/reining horse. So Paige Ranch is being built into existence as we speak."

"He has jumped into this big time after all that talk about no purpose."

"Sure has and I'm loving it. The Rocking Bar P Ranch. I didn't realize what J was feeling before. I was ready to leisurely continue life in a semi-retirement kind of way while co-managing the estate. Now with this, it seems he's evolved into the JJ I knew in California."

"That's wonderful, honey. I know that was important to you. You have known several different JJ's."

"You are so right, I have known a few different personifications of him since we all first met at the Oil Tower. Even one where I thought he was a murderer."

Rosie with a smile. "Glad that is in years past, but you must admit that you two have had a thing from the moment your relationship was accidentally bumped into being."

"It has had a few up and down, topsy-turvy moments, hasn't it?"

"Yes. He has been on a mission since he has a name for his land. I think that is the first time I've called it his land. I guess names are important to help define your environment."

"What's his mission?"

"It seems our sweet summer rain has brought construction to a halt so he has switched endeavors. He's having a split letter metal sign cut with the ranch name and brand for the entrance gate."

"Don't bother him then."

"No, what was your question?"

"I kinda wanted to see if White Oil gave him any additional information on why Matthew Driscoll wasn't interested in oil lease money."

THE WILSON FARM

"They're coming! Geri, get out here."

Geri appears by her husband's side at the south gate, the true entrance to the house. Geri straightens her dress usually worn on Sundays and Ben notices the return of a smile. Yes, a real smile and not a forced one to which he has become so accustomed. Ben misses the old Geri but maybe with her baby back home things might be better. *One can only hope...*

A white sedan with the Oklahoma Department of Corrections emblem stops and Geri watches her son exit. Jake's eyes are aglow as he and his mother connect.

"Hello, I'm Kelly Morgan, Probations and Parole Officer with Oklahoma DOC and you're?"

"We're Jake's parents, I'm Ben and this is Geraldine."

"Ben offers, "Geri, do we have the coffee on? Could we invite you in, Officer Morgan?"

Ben no. Stop talking and let him leave. Let's get Jake settled!

Officer Morgan declines but addresses Geri. "Are you alright, Mrs. Wilson?"

"Yes, fine. Maybe a little warm in the sun."

"Well, I'll be going."

Officer Morgan turns to leave and Ben asks, "What are the rules, what do we need to know?"

"Mr. Wilson, Jake is aware of the circumstances that have made his parole possible, and also the requirements of his employment, secure environment, and conditions needed to keep revocation from happening." *Not to mention influential friends.*

JAKE WILSON

"Mom, how do we get around Dad? I thought you had told him. He thinks I'm doing all the milking and he's back on the horses."

GERALDINE WILSON

"Hello Connie, I won't keep you long."

"No worries. What's up?"

"Jakes home."

"Oh Geri, you and Ben must be so relieved."

"Yes, but…"

"Does he need a few days to get acclimated? I completely understand if he does."

"No, he's anxious to come to work for you."

"Okay, tomorrow? Let's start with eight hours."

"That's great, but Ben has him helping in the barn. I was wondering, how do I put this tactfully? Would you mind speaking with Jake about your stable hand job?"

"Of course, have him give me a call."

"Well, a…that's the thing. No one knows except Jake and me about our arrangement. Connie, are you there?"

ROSIE REDMOND ROSEMAN

"You out here rocking all alone. It must be bad, no music going."

"Yup."

"Okay, Connie, tell me. Who, what, where?"

Connie with eyes closed and a heavy sigh rubs her finger between her brows as her need to continue rocking is exacerbated. "Geri Wilson, for one, then JJ."

"Geez. Start with JJ."

"I was speaking with Geri and JJ's call came up. I inadvertently hit end on Geri instead of hold. I told J that I had hung up on Geri but I could call her back. He said he hoped it had to do with the stable hands because he needed to get ranch hands. Then Rosie, do you know what he said?"

"No honey, I don't."

"He said the ranch has him so busy he lost track of time, then..."

"Yes. Okay, but you wanted him to have a purpose didn't you?"

"Uh-huh."

"Now get to the bad part."

"Then he said, with a huff, that he was busy but, he could handle it all."

"Then to top it all off, he got upset because the stable hands haven't started yet and Beauty needs attention and should he find TIME to do some calling? I told him you and I were taking perfect care of Beauty and I could have stable hands as soon as tomorrow. He said good because Beauty needs more than feed and hugs!"

Connie turns away.

"Are you crying?"

"Not exactly."

"Yes, exactly!"

"Ut oh, yup, boy oh boy, tis, tis, tis! Is it too early for wine?"

"I guess not."

"Wine and a rocker, that's better, now go on. What about Geri? If Jake isn't available don't let that upset you, I bet the Piedmont guy has friends. Yes, that will probably be better in the long run." *Please Lord, let that be it. Jake can't be the stable hand. Lord, you remember that deal with Connie about telling Pete everything? I think she is under the impression my slight nod was a yes.*

"Rosie, you know how I don't want to mislead anyone, never lie when the truth is best?"

"Yes, you have given me a comeuppance a few times. Completely deserved mind you, totally deserved. Okay, now Geri!"

"Well, listen to this. Geri is acting like she knows nothing about our arrangement or should I say her arrangement. She's the one that contacted me. She even wants me to call when they are all in the barn milking so Ben will hear the entire conversation like it has just occurred to me and what a totally fantastic idea."

"Really! How do you feel about that, Connie? A total deception, almost a lie, well actually, I think it is worse than a lie. Don't do it. That will show her that you are no one to be trifled with."

"But then…"

No, no Lord, no 'but then'!

"…Geri reminds me of Ben's desire to keep poor Jake working for the dairy which means that his probation officer will see only paystubs signed by his father. Jake has two months to report a viable job and documentation of such."

"So?"

"So, I just need to calm down before I damage our relationship. I'll make the call tomorrow bright and early when they are all milking."

Rosie thinks a nonverbal response.

JEREMIAH JASON PAIGE

"Hello, Ladies."

Connie jumps. "Where'd you come from?"

"Can't do much at the ranch with this rain, so I went to the stables to see if everything is ready for the hands you have hired."

"They won't have much to keep them busy if you can't use them."

"I'll leave a list. They can get the stables pulled together by moving all the stuff we have accumulated in the stalls. Beauty needs to be ridden daily and given a good brushing."

"Good. So the arena is underwater?"

"Pretty much but what wouldn't be after 5" of rain the last two days?

Can this ground hold one more inch of water? I said we'd take all we can get, but poor western Oklahoma looked bad when I was there. They only got a couple of inches and not enough to break the drought. The trip to Mountain View told the tale. Cattle grazing on nothing more than sparse green pasture."

"I wanted to go with you when you went to get the filly."

"Oh Connie, she's a beauty, and well worth the four hours on the road to Rainy Mountain Ranch. I got Doug's blessings and having her shipped to him for breeding with Magic."

"And Doug is sending mares?"

"Yes, this place is going to be buzzing. There is going to be a lottery and I'm hoping to have the opportunity to purchase a gray gelding to use with Beauty. The gelding is a cutting horse and will be very helpful in Beauty's growth."

"Ponies at the estate and prospects at the ranch. Prayers that our attorney can keep any legal ramifications at bay."

"Speaking of that, when the weather clears, I'll take you'll on the four wheeler. I found evidence of excavation by one of the waterfalls."

"Excavation by who? Driscolls?"

"Seems so. I don't think they knew what they were looking for because all Phillip told Matthew was that he overheard Charles say the value is in the land. Am I correct?"

"Yes."

FLAGG AND FLAGG LAW FIRM

"Connie, Richard here. The Driscolls have filed a Motion to Show Cause along with several affidavits from persons who were present when Charles agreed to return the land upon payment of the debt from Matthew. After a favorable ruling from the judge, they are going to file a Cease and Desist Order to stop any further disturbance to the land on Hefner Road."

"Richard, does JJ know?"

"I've contacted him, and he's not happy. He stated, until official notice from the court he is continuing with his endeavors."

CONSTANCE LOUISE SINCLAIR

"Another cup?"

"You have gotten me into this terrible habit."

"But it's a good one, right."

"I guess, but you never have a second cup and I always do."

Connie chuckles at Rosie's scowl.

"What do you call it?"

"Well not so much me, but JJ insinuates it's my fancy coffee. I call it my sweet delight."

"I bet he's right and it probably has as many calories as a Braum's banana split."

"I could eat one of those too," chides Connie. "You hungry?"

"Yes, always."

"Banana Split?"

"Noooo," Rosie adamantly answers.

Connie says, "I eat when I'm nervous."

"What's got your nerves in an uproar?"

Connie shrugs, "You mostly."

Rosie concedes, "Okay, let's go to town and get 'normal food'. No Braums, though."

"Guess we'll take the truck. I don't want to move Chris' car seat again." The girls load into the truck but Rosie can't get her mind off the problem at hand. Tell Pete or don't tell Pete, that was her dilemma.

Connie turns right onto 81 highway and Rosie says, "I thought we were going to El Reno to eat."

"We can if you want but Okarche is closer and we'd be backtracking to go to El Reno. We're a couple of miles from Okarche. We can eat at the Tower Cafe and bring cinnamon rolls home for tomorrow."

They top the overpass and Rosie says, "Can we drive downtown first, I've never been here."

"Sure."

In a mere three blocks, Connie turns right.

"Here it is, downtown Okarche. The town was named by taking parts of three words, Oklahoma, Arapaho and Cherokee."

"That's interesting."

"Okarche has the oldest bank in the state and Eischens, on your right, is always a busy spot. It has always been popular but several food network shows have boosted their visibility to new heights."

"Now I'm really hungry."

Rosie sees the cinnamon rolls the minute the ladies enter the Tower. Connie sits at a table by the window and watches Rosie settle Chris beside her.

Rosie gazes in the distance at the silos.

"This has got your hackles up, hasn't it? I'm sorry I can't help more. Geri and Ben have always helped and never turned away even when I thought I would lose everything. I just can't renege on my offer of employment for Jake."

"That and what your lawyer friend told you about Driscolls not wanting the land disturbed."

"Yup."

"And, why didn't Driscolls take advantage of the oil leases? Answer me that."

Rosie rubs her head, mind turning. She feels so close to pulling this all together.

"Rosie, let's sleep on it, deal?"

"Okay, deal."

Connie chatters on trying to be in the moment, while not fueling Rosie's continual need for knowledge.

"We can go back home through the country, I can show you Scott's Lake and the Selectman's place where we rescued the surrey for the kid's wedding."

Connie drives east on Main. "This side is Kingfisher County and this side is Canadian County. So I'm going to drive right down the middle of the road and guess what? We're in the same vehicle but we're in two separate counties."

Connie looks at Rosie. "Come on Rosie, that's got to be funny." But Rosie seems like a dog with a bone she has buried and forgotten where.

"Rosie, can you come and help me place these plates in the top cabinet."

"Sure. What do you have planned for today?"

"I spoke with JJ about Driscoll's latest attempt to derail our plans and he is not daunted in the least. He feels enthusiastic over the filly he has sent to Doug, and so it seems we are full steam ahead."

"Well good for him. I don't like bullies. Driscolls have used a hired bodyguard, and then this legal thing to unnerve and intimidate."

"I told him about hiring the stable workers. He was happy and reminded me I should expect to have to share them between the stables and the ranch."

"And the part about Jake being on parole was kosher with JJ?"

"That might not have come up because he was quick to remind me of the box under Charles' desk. He said if we were going to have workers I needed to do something with everything we brought home from Charles' office safe."

"I don't know that much about office stuff like filing and alphabetizing but you can tell me what to do."

Connie hands Rosie a glass of tea as the girls head to the stairs. "You don't have to worry about any of that. It's, well..."

"Well, what?"

Connie stops at the foot of the stairs, looks at Rosie with a grimace.

"Well, there's this small tape I found in the stuff. I had waited until after the kid's wedding to go through it and after they left for their honeymoon, I saw it. I don't know if it's an answering machine tape or what."

"So what's so strange about a tape besides its size?"

"What is written on it?"

"A name, I think, oh Rosie, I don't know. I don't even know how to listen to it. You'll have to look."

Rosie, now anxious, heads up the stairs as Connie forces herself to keep up. "Charles has a tape that he finds valuable enough to place in his safe. I'm intrigued!"

Rosie glances back as if waiting for instructions.

"Everything's under the desk in the alcove."

Rosie switches on the desk light. Connie moves the chair to the corner. Rosie pulls the box into the light but steps away. Connie rapidly sorts through shaking each stack of papers. "It has to be in here someplace."

A small clatter is heard as the tape hits the plastic desk mat along with a few papers.

Rosie plucks the tape from the floor. Woah, this is tiny. What's written on it? Joy?"

Connie gasps, "Joy, no I thought it said Joe."

"It isn't clear. It could say Joe. We need to find an old tape recording machine. A really small one, though."

Connie walks to the French doors, watches the Oklahoma wind have its way with the large Elm, and sighs.

"Do you know a Joy or Joe, possibly a niece or cousin?"

"No, no, no. Rosie, I can't do any more possiblies."

"That's what has you concerned, you're thinking Joy as in a female and another tryst?"

Connie places her hand over her mouth as she feels the air leave her body.

Rosie spins the chair just as Connie abruptly drops.

ROSIE REDMOND ROSEMAN

Rosie hollers from the staircase, "Connie, where are you?"

"In the kitchen. Hand me those glasses."

"Do I hear a please?"

"Okay, please."

"I thought you are going to let the hired help do this from now on. What am I saying, we both use to be the hired help. How quickly I forgot, but I must admit I like slinging those words, 'hired help' around."

"They are not hired help, Rosie. They are my friends and I treat them as such. What do you have in your hand?"

"Part of a tree. I sat down in Charles' chair and it stuck me."

"Let me see! No, it isn't part of a tree, see it has a little base. It is a tree, a miniature tree."

"Used for what?"

"Oh, it's part of the train, or I should say the scenery for the train."

"Well, it sure got my attention the moment I sat down."

"That's odd. I wonder how it got there."

"You'd think the cleaning lady would have found it."

"Or we should have. How many times have we sat there while on the computer?"

"Just drop it on the bar and I'll put it with the other stuff."

Rosie taps the tree on the counter but avoids releasing it. "Where is this other stuff?"

"In the train room."

"The train room! Haven't I been in all the rooms in this house?"

"Guess not. It's just on the other side of the laundry back to your left before you get to the pool cabana."

"Show me!"

Connie tosses the tea towel from her shoulder. "This way."

The girls hear the rain falling softly and experience a slight chill.

Connie flips on the lights as she gives a warming rub to her arms and says, "Wait here."

She walks forward, moves a chair, and locates a toggle switch. "Okay, turn the overhead lights off."

Connie flips the switch. The small village comes to life with twirling ice skaters on a frozen pond, church lights gleam through stained glass windows as one of the trains exits the tunnel and crosses a trestle.

Rosie is in awe. "This is every child's dream, Chris has to see this."

Connie takes the small evergreen from Rosie. "Charles made these," as she places the evergreen in its row with the multitude of others.

Rosie paces the length of the immense display. "He made all of this?"

"Pretty much. The foundation materials he has a patent on."

"Connie, I'm beyond impressed. Charles not only invented the filtration system for the oil wells but even made items so small and delicate with the same degree of ability."

"Yes, his mind was always at work."

Rosie immediately feels a kinship with Charles as her mind often twists, turns, and churns while rolling ideas around.

"We had some guests from Kansas and while showing them around the OKC Bombing Memorial Charles wanted to see the structural backside of the remaining wall and I remember thinking he could have been a structural engineer. That seemed to be the way he thought."

"What is Charles trying to tell us now? Have you felt him since I found the tree?"

Connie shakes her head, defeat evident.

Rosie plops in a chair, arms dangling and legs straightened to the max. "What am I missing?"

Connie stretches, walks to the far side of the room, and strokes her throat. "Maybe we are looking for something that isn't there."

Rosie spins her chair. "Nope, that prod I received from that tree led us here. What am I missing? Maybe I don't know enough about the oil business?"

"Certainly not. You see things that no one else does, Rosie. Anything adverse, objectionable or perceived negative observation peaks your interest."

Rosie looks heavenward and says, "Charles, talk to us. Oh Lord, what am I MISSING?"

Frustration takes the lead as Rosie throws her hands in the air in an 'I give up' gesture.

Connie walks forward to emit some uplifting words just as Rosie pummels the tabletop with her fist.

Connie is forced to back a few paces as objects and apparatus fly helter-skelter with one resolutely landing squarely at Rosie's feet, although in pieces.

Rosie apologizes while picking up the plastic sections. Connie grabs items from behind. Rosie, now with great ascertain makes space for reassembly.

Connie says, "Charles is here."

Rosie whispers, "Thank you, Lord."

"Connie, this is it. Give me what you have. Yes, this is it. I need one more piece. The plastic lid or maybe not. I bet it will work without the top closure. Don't you see the tape is from an answering machine and possibly this very one. Where's the cord? Need a CORD!"

JAKE WILSON

"Mrs. Sinclair, this is Jake. I'm sorry if this is too early to call. We're in the barn milking."

"Hello, Jake. You've never called me Mrs. Sinclair, please don't start now."

"Okay. Connie. Mother suggested I verify my starting date."

"You tell me, Jake."

"No, you."

Connie feels the tension even on the phone. Was his father listening?

"Monday is fine."

"Okay, thank you, Mrs. Sinclair. Monday it is."

Jake thinks, *I jumped at parole but can I do it, can I betray Connie?*

CONSTANCE LOUISE SINCLAIR

"Rosie, the recorder adaptor has been delivered."

"Thank you, Amazon. Let's pray it fits. Meet you in the kitchen?"

"Yes, I'll grab the stuff. Pleeazzee fit. It fits. Sit here!"

"I'm good standing. Rosie, don't look at me that way, just hit play."

"Connie, I can assure you this is not evidence of an affair."

A whirl is heard, tape rewinds, then. "Who is this Connie? Who's talking?"

"Charles. Shush."

Okay Mother, start again so I can get all this down.

Mother Sinclair told me…

And who is Mother Sinclair?

Charles, you know!

Yes, I do. Mother Sinclair is Jessie Sinclair my grandmother and she told you…

Oh Charles, she wanted nothing more than you to be happy and have her some greats. She waited…

I know, Mother. Connie and I tried to fulfill her wish.

Marriage and children are always assumed.

I love Connie so much, so very much.

229

Connie leans in, she feels Charles, and her resolve to stand and stay detached, melts. "I love you, too, baby."

Connie sits and hits rewind, not once but multiple times, as Charles proclaims his love.

Rosie stops the tape to comfort her friend. "Are you okay, do we need to take a break?"

Connie retrieves a tissue and nods as she again sits.

'Mother Sinclair told me her father would often sit on the grand porch with his family and tell of a time when water would be as valuable as gold. He told of calling his brother to come help him divine for water.'

'Do you remember his name?'

'Of course, Cecil Sinclair. He lived in Lawton and divined many wells in that area.'

'Go on.'

'She said that the well hit big and the well water tested high quality.'

'Yes, when you first told me I called about a WQI test which is an indicator that tests the water quality...and that's where our problem lies.'

'Exactly.'

'Are we done? Turn it off.'

'No, tell how they stored the paperwork. Surely, there are papers showing testing. If we can locate the well source I think I may be able to create a filtration system for the water well.'

'Mother Sinclair told me she had memories of glass milk jars being stored in the cellar on their farm north of El Reno. Each jar held one year's worth of papers needed for taxes. She was adamant that one of the jars had pertinent information worth looking into. But, Charles, I never put any stock into any of this and you shouldn't either.'

'You just tell me, Mom, it's my job to find the nexus.'

'Why glass jars?'

'Well Charles, you can't just put things in the cellar because of the moisture and rodents.'

'So there are gallon milk jugs somewhere on their farm?'

'Yes, I've seen a picture of them setting on a small concrete walk next to a cellar, well at least six to eight of them. But Charles, it's not ours any longer.'

'I remember, Grandpa wagered it in a buggy race and lost.'

"Connie, get your keys, we're headed to the Court House."

ROSIE REDMOND ROSEMAN

"So the land is the same. The farm north of town that Jessie's father wagered and lost is the OK Sportsman's Club. How ironic that the Sinclair's lost it in a race and Charles regained it through a race."

"If Magic had been in the buggy race it wouldn't have been lost in the first place," Connie declares.

SINCLAIR STABLES

Mike Dixon considers his options. Keep this job with all the ramifications it incurs or quit now before he is pulled in more deeply. On the plus side, the monetary benefits of dual employers are tempting.

"Hey, sounds like you're in the car?"

"Yes, Rosie and I are headed home from town. What about you? You done for the day?"

"Well, yes and no. I have one more contractor here working at the arena on the electric but then shutting down until the rain stops and it dries up some."

"Oh, great. You coming to the estate now?"

"Not yet, I want to call on the ranch sign then do a walk-through at the lodge. All the locks have been rekeyed and the security system changed over and upgraded with cameras. Then I can switch to working at the lodge until the weather swings back our direction. What's for dinner?"

"Haven't gotten that far yet, but something filling and warm to take the chill off seems good."

"Fried potatoes, goulash, salad, and fresh bread?"

"Yes sir. Sounds perfect so you cooking?" Connie adds with a chuckle.

"Wait, Rosie wants to say something."

"JJ, would you mind terribly if we stop by and see the improvements you've made."

"Fine, I'll wait for you at the arena office."

"No, we'll meet you at the Lodge."

"Oh, yeah, Connie."

"What, J?"

"You can tell your attorney that the Cease and Desist Order didn't make it on time. The well is producing."

JAKE WILSON

"Hey, you all. I start at Connie's Monday."

"Okay, so I can cook you a hardy breakfast and then see you at lunch."

"No, I'm packing a lunch. And Mom, I'll be working some late nights so don't worry about holding supper for me."

ROSIE REDMOND ROSEMAN

"Have we missed the turn?"

"No, it's the second road east after we cross the river. Do you think the bottles could be in the cellar where we were held?"

"No, unless they are buried. The police gave that place the once over twice."

"The same police that missed everything in Ludlow's office?"

"Is there a cellar in the lodge?"

"I would think so, even if only for wine. What are you thinking, Rosie? I know that look. Your mind is working."

"I love it when it all starts coming together, and I also hate it. Decisions, girl, girl, girl. I'm thinking we need to get in the lodge when JJ isn't present."

"Rosie, not happening. I'm not rocking this boat again. You know how explosive my past betrayals have been. Remember, full disclosure. Besides, Charles didn't want JJ to go to California and we still don't know why."

"Yeah, yeah."

Connie strains to look in the rearview mirror and sees Chris is content.

Rosie leans around and Chris gives a big smile, then starts flailing his arms and kicking his feet. "I'm glad he is old enough to finally front face in his car seat."

"Kids grow so fast."

"Yes, he certainly has, but Connie, we can't go to the lodge."

"Why?"

"I can guarantee you that sweet smile won't last long enough for us to get him in his stroller. It will be time for him to eat. Isn't that right big boy?"

The flailing and kicking returns.

"Hey, you beat us!"

"Yes, I did. I've got the hard part done. Potatoes peeled, sliced, and in the skillet and your water is on for the macaroni."

Rosie places Chris in his highchair. "Let me feed my hungry child and I can make the salad."

"Wine, anyone?"

"Of course. Listen to that rain. Thank you, Lord, for your rain, which we don't get to enjoy in the summertime, often."

"I heard from the kids today."

"How's everything at the ranch? J, you know, we have two ranches now so we need to delineate."

"The kids don't know that. I'm waiting on the sign to be delivered and hung before I reveal the name to them."

"Is that soon and have you sent pictures of the arena since it's covered?"

"Yes, and the offices with the full bank of windows positioned so that our clients can stay comfortable while watching their horses being exercised and trained."

It isn't unnoticed by Connie that he includes her in recognition of their clients.

"Oh, and what's up with obtaining BLM horses."

"I've gone a full 360 degree on that. You don't remember, but qualifications through the Bureau of Land Management are very time-consuming. I was gone for weeks not to mention locating reputable drivers with trucks to transport. Then the veterinarian certs and the list goes on and on."

"Do you want to hit some local sale barns or even out of state? There is a huge horse sale in Wyoming. We'd have to look up the dates. Might have already missed it. And…" Connie states, to draw attention to her upcoming statement. "And, let's not forget that Rich Strike was bought through a lottery."

"You are dreaming big now, but Doug and I are talking the horse situation over. I want to get mares from him and use Magic but it will have to be by AI as Doug doesn't trust the wild mares even penned and with our own ranch hands. He's the expert and can pick the ponies without transporting them to him or even worse, online."

Rosie places the cutting mat on the counter with the romaine. "I would think it would be hard for Doug to deny your request even though he and Amanda are full owners of Magic. How much is a gift of half a racehorse, anyway?" Followed by a more than demonstrative tsk, tsk, tsk.

"See JJ, even Rosie is missing ponies, and you had me anticipating ponies like the California ponies."

"Let me see what I can do. But my main goal is to have the arena finished before horses."

"How long on the lodge?"

Connie notices that Rosie has stopped making the salad, and has even stepped toward their conversation.

"JJ is the lodge grand. I'm so anxious to see it," quips Rosie.

"Yes it is. Whoever the builder was he took pride in his work. It was quite stately and imposing in its day. It faces northwest to maximize the view. The logs have been beveled to help with the overall aesthetics and held together with ½" cables. Upon entering off the sizeable porch into the entrance hall which is 100' by 80' the enormous stone fireplace takes your eye upward the full height of both stories, I'm thinking at least 60'. The lofty ceiling is all wood decking. On the left side of the main floor is the kitchen and eating area I plan on turning into an onsite café. On the right side is a 20' room I think was used as the gun room. Then there is an observation room to watch the skeet range and trap shooting competitions."

Connie says, "What fun this is going to be."

"That reminds me, when do the stable hands start?"

"Monday, and only our one little pony."

"I don't even know who you've hired. Have I met them before?"

"I'm not sure. One is Jake Wilson. Could you pass the bread," Connie asks trying to stall for time. "And then, I also hired Mike Dixon. He lives between here and Piedmont so he's fairly close. It will be convenient for him. He's married. Very dependable. I don't know if he has kids or not...

"Woah, back up. I know I don't know Mike Dixon but the first???

"Oh, yes, Jake Wilson you know Geri and Ben's son?"

"Yes, I know about Jake and how can you hire him if he is in prison?"

"Rosie, pass the butter, I love fresh bread."

"Connie?"

Rosie thinks, *Oh, girl, girl, girl.*

Connie says, "Look at that sweet child. He's asleep in his high chair."

Rosie rises, and without making eye contact with either, says, "Oh my, I'll get him in his jammies."

"Jake, glad you made it home before we turned in."

"Where's Dad?"

"Went back to the barn. We've got two cows with swollen utters so he's seeing to them. Here."

"What's this?" Jake takes the manila envelope and looks for any company lettering or return address.

"Some guy dropped it off for you."

"Did he leave a name?"

"No, but Dad said he was a friend of yours."

"Really?"

"Yup. You know anyone that drives a dark blue SUV. He said the metal tag holder had Yukon in the very center of it."

"Amanda, did you talk to JJ? My voicemail says to call him ASAP."

"JJ, what's up?"

"I need horses."

"I thought you were going with BLM?"

"No, I'm not spending the time and effort on that again, and I don't dare be away from here right now."

"What's the problem?"

"Doug, I have been pushing Connie to get stable hands for us to share at the estate and the ranch so she's hired two. I don't know one of them, but the other is the neighbor kid who has just been paroled."

"The Wilson boy?"

"Yes."

"I've never met him, but, JJ, just say no."

"You'd think I could, but between me almost demanding workers and Connie making a promise to Geri, well…she's not backing down. She won't go back on the deal. Doug, I need horses to keep these guys busy. You need to ship me horses. It doesn't matter if it's just the culls or what. I need horses!"

ROSIE REDMOND ROSEMAN

"Sorry I ran out on you last night. I'll confess, I was never a fan of Jake working here. It's better this way."

"No, Rosie, that's not what happened. I can't go back on my word. Jake has to work here. His probation agreement says gainful employment within two months and we're past that. I can't be the reason he returns to prison. And, JJ knows about the tape conversation between Charles and his mother. He is in agreement on that part. He will be helping us figure this out."

JEREMIAH JASON PAIGE

"Hello gentlemen, I'm JJ Paige and I will be your contact person at the estate and the ranch. There is never an appropriate reason to be at the house or near the ladies. If this is a problem, now is the time to speak up!"

CONSTANCE LOUISE SINCLAIR

"Rosie, do you think we can bundle Chris and meet JJ at the ranch?"

"I guess, do you know what the temperature is?"

"It's 69, but the rain has moved all east of us. Sun should be out soon."

"Arena or lodge?"

"I didn't ask, although I imagine the lodge. The arena will be flooded, but we can walk through the offices and client viewing area."

ROSIE REDMOND ROSEMAN

"So how does the key deal work?"

"Well, the north gate stays open during work hours and there are only certain areas in the stables that need keys, tack room, feed room, storage…"

"No, I know about the estate, I mean the ranch?"

"To tell you the truth, I have no idea. I don't even know if the white pipe gate at the entrance is still in use…Oh my, hold on Rosie."

"Oh, geez."

Connie feels Charles at the exact moment the speeding car careens, makes a 180, and comes to a stop with one back tire in the ditch. Rosie is unbuckled and almost in the back seat with Chris as Connie sits frozen. The mud flies, and the driver frees his car and speeds off.

The girls chatter on about the incident as they top the last hill on Hefner, each gasp as they see JJ's jeep on its side, steam rising.

KIRBY KERMAN

"Hello Boss, you'd think this guy would be home during a rain storm."

"This is the perfect opportunity to set a fire with the arena being new, potential faulty wiring or a lightning strike. Keep trying."

"I'm fine officer, and the ladies and baby are okay as well."

"Were they involved?"

"No."

"Dispatch, no ambulance needed at my location." The officer radio's using his lapel mic.

"But I do want to file a complaint."

"Can you give me a description of the vehicle?"

"It was a dark blue SUV, to tell you the truth with the cloud cover, and spitting rain, its headlights were the first thing I noticed as it approached because he adjusted them to bright."

"So, it was a male."

"I can't say for sure. It happened so fast. He just veered into me and I took a defensive measure that flipped me into the ditch."

"JJ, I think you're right, it was dark blue. I was gonna say black," Rosie injects.

JJ and the officer speak in unison, "What?"

Connie pipes in, "Yes, it was blue, and I got a tag number! Well, a partial one."

Rosie not to be outdone, "I got one too."

Connie says, "It was DSW 2 something."

"No," says Rosie, it was GSW 24 something."

"No, it was DSW just like the initials for Discount Shoe Warehouse."

"No, it was GSW, you know? Gunshot wound."

"Sir, you didn't tell me there were witnesses."

"Headquarters to 13."

"Go ahead."

"Captain wants to know if you need assistance."

"Not at this time." Then in a lowered voice says, "I've kinda got a Thelma and Louise situation goin' on here."

CONSTANCE LOUISE SINCLAIR

J, while you're waiting on the wrecker, Rosie and I are taking Chris to the offices at the arena, or is the lodge open?

ROSIE REDMOND ROSEMAN

"Connie, keep going. Don't stop here."

"You mean to keep going to the lodge?"

"Yup. I know what you are going to say, but we aren't intentionally bypassing JJ. He said it's not locked, so that's an invitation of sorts."

Just then, the radiance of the afternoon sun illumines the lodge as if from a thousand suns.

"Rosie, how spectacular. God has curated this moment for us. Yes, the lodge it is."

Connie lifts the front of Chris' stroller as they skillfully advance the steps.

Rosie thinks the immense double doors are twice her height. She steps forward, the rays light the fireplace stones as if penetrating the door before it's even opened.

Connie twirls the stroller as she thinks this has to be a refuge from ages past.

"Rosie, I wish I had seen this in its wilder days. Can't you just imagine? Stop and listen."

"What?"

"Listen to the sounds of the prior time resonate. The untamed chaos, the heaviness of smoke lingering in the rafters, the rawness of the moment. Energy that can't be restricted. Prattle, some verbose, among drinkers looking for a sanctuary as they haphazardly spill the contents in their hands to and fro. Can't you feel the rawness yet innocence of the bygone life?"

"I guess," Rosie states as she unceremoniously turns accepting Connie's challenge to inhale the imperceptible, which at this moment was not obvious, clear, or palpable.

"Connie, get your head out of the clouds. Have you forgotten why we are here? Look around."

"I know. This will be a costly renovation, code regulations, and rising cost of materials, if they are even available, but thank you, Lord, it can all be met through the now producing well. It's all you, God. The key to everything is the oil production."

"HELLO Connie, we're here looking for milk jugs."

"Okay, okay. JJ said the kitchen is to the left. Surely the cellar entry will be off the kitchen. Where are the lights? No sunshine in this hall."

Rosie skirts Connie and Chris and with a flick lights reveal the kitchen. The east wall has two double door refrigerators with counter and cabinets extending to a large convection oven.

Connie runs her hands over the stainless doors of the oven as Chris starts to climb out of his stroller. Connie picks him up and says, "No you don't. You're not touching this floor."

"I can take him."

"No, he's good. See, he just wanted to touch these oven doors. Chris, I bet you are going to be a great cook someday."

"If he takes after his father, he surely will be."

To the left and center of the kitchen is the workstation complete with a Hobart dishwasher. Connie carries Chris to a matching Hobart mixer and stainless bowl.

"Look Rosie, this thing is so big I could put Chris in there and not even see him. This kitchen is meant for some serious cooking."

At the far end are two wooden doors. Rosie opens them with caution, pulls a string hanging in front of her, and sees the butler's pantry loaded with dishes, serving platters, and numerous glasses.

"Yup, they have the serving pieces to accommodate that mixer."

Rosie turns and sees, between the pantry and at the end of the refrigerators a door.

"Connie, here it is. I bet this is it."

Connie joins Rosie. Rosie grasps the handle to open, but steps back as the door doesn't open into the kitchen it opens away. Rosie glances Connie's way, and Connie with a shrug and partial nod says, "Go on."

The door partially opens just as JJ enters. "What are you doing up here? Look at me. Do you know how far I had to walk? Where are your phones, anyway? Let's go it has started raining again."

CONSTANCE LOUISE SINCLAIR

Connie stands and looks down at the bench where she has been seated, but for how long. Time seems to have escaped her. Connie removes her shoes as she so often does preferring either the coolness of the grass or as in this time to walk where the sweet summer rain has lightly imposed itself on the edge of the lanai.

She notices one small ring of concrete in which the cooling water was not able to encroach. To some extent, Connie can relate. What exactly was she feeling?

JJ's entry and behavior at the lodge was disconcerting leaving Connie flustered by a less-than-ideal situation. But this is not a new feeling. JJ has disregarded Connie's ideas, opinions, and choices, and sometimes even with a dismissive gesture.

This hostility, or maybe that is too strong of a word, but certainly, argumentativeness, between us seems to have stemmed from Doug and Amanda's wedding. JJ had made it plain, even though in a joking manner, that their alone time had been too few and far in between.

Was this uneasiness bleeding over into her decision making? Is she disturbed over her inability to see a clear course of action? Surely JJ remembers their previous conversation standing in front of the fireplace after they had returned from the Wilsons where Geri insinuated JJ was my gentleman friend.

Connie enters the house through the sunroom but before going into the kitchen, stops to admire her beautiful orchids now covered in blooms.

She places her hand on the freezer door and sees proclaimed upon the attached magnet, 'Be still and know that I am God!'

I'm trying Lord, I'm trying, please show me the way.

ROSIE REDMOND ROSEMAN

"Pete's home tomorrow."

"Rosie, I bet you can't wait to get home."

"A little alone time with my big guy is extremely tempting."

"I can tell."

"Do you think we can push JJ into taking us back to the lodge first thing in the morning?"

"You don't stop do you?"

"Stop what?"

"Stop thinking!"

"No, because JJ said he had located where excavation had occurred on the far side of the property. I think JJ is right. The Driscolls have no idea what they are looking for."

"As if we do."

"Connie, don't give up that easy."

SINCLAIR STABLES

"Hey, Jake. You're late again. Do you think just because your family is on first name basis you can slack off?"

Jake shoots a look Mike's way.

"Besides you missed all the hubbub."

"Like what?"

"I guess JJ was run off the road and flipped his new Rubicon. Can you imagine just getting to drive that sweet ride much less own a Jeep Rubicon?"

"I bet Connie was upset. But the other guy's insurance should cover it."

"Nope just veered directly for him and left. The only thing for certain is it was a dark blue SUV of some type."

JEREMIAH JASON PAIGE

"Here, catch," JJ says. "You go on to the Lodge. I have to make a run into town and I don't want Rosie to be late meeting Pete."

"We're not exactly ready, either. Waiting on Madison to get here to watch Chris."

Rosie chuckles, "Not much watching to do. She'll have him in the train room enthralled for hours."

THE ROCKING BAR P RANCH

Connie stops the car after the short drive up the ranch entrance road.

"Will you look at that! Not so little."

"And the cut metal trees and racing horses make for a perfect sign."

"Do you think your feller knows exactly what he wants or what?"

The gates open, but Connie doesn't drive through. Rosie releases her seatbelt and turns in her friend's direction.

"Okay, what's wrong? Do you need to talk?"

"No, not until you said that," Connie replies while releasing a short gasp.

"What, about JJ knowing exactly what he wants?"

"Oh Rosie, up until JJ took on the development of this property he was…what are the words I'm looking for. He was tentative about his position at the estate. I never told you, the only real fights JJ and I have had has been over him feeling vulnerable. At the attorney's office, over his address being the same as mine. When we found the deeds to the California land. When Geri usurped his authority as she downplayed his offered hand and called him 'gentlemen friend'."

"Woah. Hold on. You did step in to bolster him, didn't you?"

277

"Well, no. Not exactly. He knows he is valued."

"Uh-huh."

"But then, listen to this. The other night, you noticed, I'm certain, JJ almost ordered us to the car. And his distaste over me not having the stable hands hired and ready."

"So he's a little frustrated."

"He knows he's appreciated."

"You think he does? I don't know much about men but I do know one thing. Pete wants and needs to feel needed and he does that by contributing everything to his family."

"I know Rosie, he is a good provider."

"Let's look at JJ's list. JJ, lost everything when he sold out to try and rescue you from the mess Charles left you in. No offense, Charles, if you're listening. Then he bought half of Magic and gave that to you. Every penny he had went to let you know that he cherished you to the point of bankrupting himself. Now that's gone as a gift to the kids. You see my point?"

With slumped shoulders and lowered head, Connie concedes.

"Soon as I'm out of here, you know what you need to do?"

"No, what."

"The same thing I did to Pete before he ask me to marry him, hang on his arm and listen intently to whatever he thinks is important. Keep the romance alive and…"

"And what?"

"Well, I think you were too comfortable when JJ was uncomfortable, and when JJ is comfortable you are uncomfortable, and you don't know how to handle it."

Rosie with clasp hands pressed against her lips closes her eyes and in a commanding voice continues, "Connie, there are storms before the rainbow, and dark clouds before the silver lining. Our lives are connected like day and night. So with joy comes sorrow, and sometimes a great sorrow, but you can't have one without the other."

Rosie looks straight at Connie. "I know what you are thinking. What control do we have? None, but without the pain, you can never truly love another. Connie are you ready to endanger this relationship?"

BETTY'S FLOWERS AND GIFTS

Conversations sputter to a halt, eyes turn, feet shuffle, and congregate at the shop window. A cat call hastily summons a curious shopper who rapidly brushes the fern fronds out of her line of sight. With a cached breath, all are cognizant as the cowboy's boot appears. Eyes move up the extended leg as it merges with the second. All minds, although following different paths, halts at his tousled hair. Silence is difficult to maintain as JJ's long fingers brush his wayward tresses from his eyes.

THE LODGE

Shadows loom, as the sun is well to the east of the lodge entrance. Connie fumbles to locate the lock and open the door. They enter the darkened room and search for the light that was not needed on their prior visit.

Connie, in a temporary moment of regret, wishes they had waited on JJ. Rosie forges forward, past the gigantic fireplace, down the hall, and enters the kitchen.

Connie halts and places her hand on the cold stainless steel door of the refrigerator. Rosie opens the basement door, continues down and feels for the switch.

"Connie, come on."

They descend, stopping at the landing, where the stairs turn.

Rosie sees the vastness of the area. "This might take longer than the time I have. Looks like it covers the full footage of the upper level. There must have been a pile of dirt that came out of here."

Connie still cautious wants to kick herself for not gaining any of Rosie's veracity during their previous events.

Shelving lines the walls and extends in rows from the back wall forward. Rosie sees the grime and says, "We didn't wear wipables."

"Wipables?"

"Yes, clothes that I can wipe the stuff off my hands, like our smocks at the Oil Tower."

"That's all can goods for use in the kitchen."

"What's back there?"

Connie pulls a box forward and sees file folders. "This looks like gun range records."

Rosie nods as she walks forward and darkness advances.

Connie searches her pocket for her phone. "Wait until I get some light. Over here, Rosie."

They lean in as the ceiling rafters dramatically lower. Unease and mental apprehension are felt with every breath. Before logical decisions can be made there it is a worn door with a hasp closure.

"Please don't have a padlock. I don't have time for a locked door. Connie, give me some light. Okay, good, just has a clasp."

Rosie adeptly removes the clip, and turns for Connie to enter. Connie takes a step back and hands Rosie her phone.

"Hey babe, what are you doing answering Doug's phone?"

"We're in the truck and he's out opening the gate."

"What? That role has changed. You were the one to open the gates when I was there."

"I know, but that was when I was a kid."

JJ laughs a hearty laugh. "You know what? You will always be that kid to me."

"Hello JJ. Glad you called, I'm just about ready to ship you some horses to help with your circumstances."

"That's great Doug, but…"

"But what? You better not be telling me you don't want them after all I've done to get them sorted."

"No. Am I on speaker?"

"Yes, but I can take you off."

"No. Amanda might be of help on this one."

"Okay."

"I've got a problem. Connie and I have been on the outs."

"Oh, J. no."

"Not bad, at least not as bad as the prior times. I've just been a little short tempered and Pete's home today so Rosie and Chris are going home so, I'm wanting to make amends and was wondering. Well Amanda, close your ears. Doug, I was wondering what you would do if you were in this situation?"

Doug reaches across the console and takes Amanda's hand. "JJ, you've got Amanda covering her eyes. Don't worry baby, I'll keep it above board."

Amanda shakes her head as a big smile of remembrance flushes her cheeks.

"Okay, I'll tell you what has worked for us twice so I know it will work for you, hopefully, once."

"Tell me."

"Find a secluded area, turn on some soft music, and dance. JJ, I'm telling you no words are needed."

"Great. Thanks. I just stopped and got flowers and candy, too."

Amanda elbows Doug. "Flowers and candy!!"

ROSIE REDMOND ROSEMAN

"I've got to get out of here, Pete's probably beat me home. Get JJ to help you or send one of the ranch hands to grab the jars. No, on second thought, don't. What happened to 6 or 8 jugs? There are a couple of dozen if not more."

"Okay, I got it, Rosie."

Rosie exits the car, opens the back door, and unbuckles Chris. She reaches into her purse and pulls out Pete's itinerary for the day.

"I don't know why I'm looking at this because Pete has already landed."

"Drive safe."

"I will, I'm just relieved we found them." Rosie looks up and says, "Thank you, Charles," as she stuffs the papers back in her purse.

THE SINCLAIR STABLES

Jake backs further into the shadows to make sure he remains undetected. He shouldn't even be here as he had clocked out hours ago. But his determination has paid off. Finally, he has something to convey. He isn't even certain who he speaks to, only a number, but if he had to guess it is the SUV driver. Up until now, the weeks at the ranch and the estate had turned up nothing. His employer, at first, wanted times on when the ranch would be vacant, but that had been impossible to determine as the one attempt to enter the land ended with JJ in the ditch.

His next assignment was to locate a waterfall and take pictures of the area to the west. That also, could not be accomplished, because JJ kept tight reins on Jake, while Mike was sent on simple errands.

Jake walks the length of the stables, jumps the fence into the paddocks, then north.

"Hello, this is Jake."

"I know who it is. What do you have for me? It better be worth my time."

"Well, yes sir, it is. Connie dropped her friend at her car and they had been to the lodge. The friend had papers and said she was relieved they had found them."

"The friend, that redhead?"

"Yes."

THE SINCLAIR ESTATE

JJ hears the entry chime and stands. Connie enters, sees the flowers, candy, and carafe of wine. She is anticipatory, but with hopeful expectations. She glances at the clock and eagerly snatches the card.

Connie, I can't wait to hold you.
All my love,
JJ

Music wafts in the distance. JJ kisses her neck. Connie quakes at the return of forgotten feelings, yes, and the desolate feelings that have been missing until now.

They dance.

JJ is overcome with chills... Is it Charles? Charles can you be giving your blessing and relinquishing Connie? JJ says a silent prayer of thanks as he hopefully grasps the moment. Finally once and for all their moment.

CONSTANCE LOUISE SINCLAIR

The night has not been Connie's friend. Connie rises, slips on a tee and shorts. She turns her bedroom handle to silently close her door. She walks a few steps past Amanda's room and sees no indication that JJ is awake. She heads downstairs, glances into the kitchen, but passes by. What has her unsettled?

Connie switches on the outside flood lights and watches the water system methodically do its job. She enters the gallery, sees her bible on the table, picks it up, and holds it to her.

Connie does the only thing that ever clears her mind and brings her peace. Connie lowers herself to her knees and prays. Lord, you know all things. You know every beat of our heart, every hair on our head. Make my path clear because Father, I don't know the way. If JJ and I aren't meant to be together, place a roadblock. I can't continue fighting these waves of emotions, our disorganized existence, so I give this to you, Lord.

Connie leans forward and buries her face in a pillow as she braces for her future.

JEREMIAH JASON PAIGE

"What are you doing up? Have you even been to bed? The outside lights are on, is there anything wrong? Connie, are you okay?"

Connie, suddenly alert, feels a sense of caution. She knows that gut feeling that heightens her awareness pushes her, and forces her to think.

"Connie, what is it?"

JJ feels confused. He turns, but why he is not sure because he knows the alarm is still set. JJ cuts his eyes back to Connie and in a placating voice, continues.

"Sweetheart, why are you on the floor?"

Connie takes a deep breath and exhales in more of a huff than she meant.

JJ continues with his questioning determined to get to the crux of the matter before things escalate.

"Are you not well? Let me help you up."

Connie finds her footing and slides onto the ottoman.

JJ sees the wariness in Connie's eyes and feels her hesitation that he thought cannot be possible after last night.

"Connie, what has happened in the few short hours since our dance? You realize that we have not danced like that in years only one other time and that was on that small dance floor in the city. Do you remember Connie?"

JJ goes to his knees and searches Connie's face, and not wanting to feel another tentative moment doesn't offer to touch her but lays a hand over his heart.

"Connie, I'm yours. Am I enough, Connie? Am I enough? Do you want me as I want you?"

"Sometimes, I think I shouldn't?"

"Why? Tell me, please look at me and tell me why?

"J it is our rollercoaster way of life. Your complacency with status quo and my complicity in letting you."

Connie diverts her eyes.

"So that's it, you don't want me anymore?"

"I don't know, oh Lord, I don't know."

JJ moves closer and now on one knee takes her hand and places it over his heart.

"Connie, every beat you feel only beats because we are together. I cannot live without you. Is it enough, am I enough, do you still want me?"

Connie turns looks into his velvet brown eyes, and places her hand upon his.

"How many times? How much longer can we do this? I don't know, maybe I shouldn't want you, but, Lord help me, I do, I do want you?"

ROSIE REDMOND ROSEMAN

"Have you gotten the bottles?"

"No."

"Well hop to it."

"Rosie…"

"Oh, Connie. What's wrong? I know that voice. What's happened? I've only been gone less than a day."

"I've been up most of the night."

"When JJ left us and we went to the lodge, he, evidently went into El Reno and got candy, flowers, wine, and a card. The minute I dropped you and Chris off and entered, there it all was."

"Aah, that was sweet, so what has you so upset?"

"His off again, on again behavior. He gets upset at situations that put him in an unbecoming light, but then we have one of the moments like last night, where all is right once more. You see don't you?"

"What I see is what we talked about before. The two of you can't seem to be at the same place at the same time. Connie, I think you need to make your mind up. Is this how you want to spend the rest of your life? I know I'm asking almost the impossible but look into the future. Do you see you two together as a married couple or if not, you need to figure out if you can walk this path unmarried but together."

JEREMIAH JASON PAIGE

"Connie, the trucks have arrived. They are offloading what Doug has sent for the ranch and then they are headed to the estate to unload the rest. I've sent the ranch hands I hired from El Reno your way until we can get some hired closer to the estate."

Connie feels Charles' presence. Oh, Charles, I'm so confused.

"Connie, I know it has only been a short time since the horses arrived, and I've waited since our last conversation. But I can't stand it. How is Beauty taking to his service horse? Has she taught him anything?"

"Yes, yes, and yes. They were the first horses to use the ranch arena. When I got there they were still dragging the arena to prepare the ground. Misty and her rider enter holding Beauty's lead. It was evident the ranch hands had done their job because as soon as Beauty was mounted he immediately started working. "

"That makes me so happy. Doug got to see it all but I wasn't on the skype call and no one thought to video it for me. Men!"

"Everything else going good?"

"Seems to be besides me missing you around her."

"Well, you have that sweet little chunk to love on don't you?"

"Oh, you mean Chris. Yes, he is such a happy baby, and we enjoyed having them at the estate."

"But all else, okay?"

"We're all well, yes."

ROSIE REDMOND ROSEMAN

"Guess who's walking? Pete is on cloud nine and I'm on my feet all the time following him, and he's in constant movement."

"Did you tag me?"

"No, not putting any public videos out, but, I'll text you them."

"How exciting. You did see my text on the bottles successful retrieval."

"No. When, how?"

"It wasn't that big of a deal. JJ got heavy-duty lawn bags, we wrapped them in paper and hauled them out."

"What's the count?"

"Twenty-seven. They are at the far end of the stables. The guys set up two long tables and I'll sort through them."

"So the hands know they are there. They're locked away though?"

"Yes, they are secure but the stable hands were gone when we made the move."

"I can't get all this out of my mind, even while I'm keeping Chris out of trouble I find my mind talking to itself."

"The bottles contents should help to enlighten us, but I know you are anxious."

"Yes, anxious from afar is the problem."

"Rosie, make your list like you have done so often, remember as you watched the recording of our intruder you made a list, as you thought through the night at the oil tower, you made a list, as you watched the Enid film of the guy who purchased the burner phone, you made a list."

"Okay, okay, you've made your point, but all of those times were at my leisure, and leisure is not a word you throw around lightly with a toddler."

PETER ROSEMAN

"Danny, I shouldn't be long. I just have to run by our place and then I will meet Rosie at the doctor's office."

"Rosie, I'm running a little late. Do you still need me to go by the apartment?"

"Yes, but don't rush, they haven't even called us back yet. Just grab those two prescription bottles on the lower shelf."

"Okay."

"Oh Pete, I didn't set the alarm so that will save you some time."

Pete enters the apartment just like the other hundreds of times, but this time he stops in the entry hall as the smell of cigarettes inundates him. With gun drawn, Pete steps into the hall glances into the bathroom, and both directions. He swiftly returns to the entryway as the master bedroom door is closed.

Pete reaches for his phone to call for backup but has to abandon the call as Pete hears the unmistakable sound of the floorboards in front of their room. His choices are to enter the kitchen in two short steps or exit the apartment which will be a longer distance. Pete backs the two steps as he sees the shadow cross the bathroom doorway. Then, with a flash of metal, shots ring out.

THE SINCLAIR ESTATE

"Rosie, what are you doing here and in a patrol car?"

"Pete has been shot at."

Connie rubs her arms.

"How horrible, but Pete's okay. That's all that matters. Come here you are shaking. Please, sit down."

Rosie frantically looks for Chris.

"He's right here. See, behind the settee. I'm watching him."

Connie makes a call.

"Madison, this is Connie Sinclair. Could you come and help with Chris? Oh, thank you so much."

"Rosie, coffee or tea?"

Connie carries Chris to the kitchen and places him on an upside- down stew pot.

"This will work until I can get your booster out."

Rosie rummages in the diaper bag and pulls out snacks and Chris' sippy cup.

Rosie sits beside Chris and nestles her hot coffee in her hands. Her shakes subside.

"Connie, Pete could have died and it's all my fault."

"Do you think…?" Connie starts to debunk Rosie's concern.

"Don't you. Who else could it be? And don't say Pete's job. I might have believed that when the intruder entered but not now. No, not now. I about got Pete killed."

"Oh, Rosie no. No, you didn't. Pete is a trained detective and that's why this had a positive outcome. Pete understood the situation. That's the reason and the only reason."

"You know the week or two before Pete got back when he called and ask if I had set the alarm."

"Yes."

"The neighbor across the street had seen on his doorbell a man in a hoodie right under our bedroom window trying to look in."

"Oh my."

"Connie, you know when you said full disclosure. No more secrets and I nodded in agreement."

"No Rosie. You never told Pete?"

"No, and that's why I said I almost got him killed. I almost got my husband murdered."

"Connie feels Charles."

PETER ROSEMAN

"Rosie, slow down. I understand you want me at Connie's, but I just called to make sure you and Chris were okay. I have paperwork to do and even if I wanted to come right now, that would be impossible. This is an officer involved shooting, and our place is a crime scene. I have to make a report and that's only after I am debriefed. I have to go."

"Pete listen. Please just listen. It's that intruder guy. Kirby Kerman was the one that pushed Connie and me into the cellar. It's him."

"Okay, okay. I have to go."

"No, Pete…Pete?"

JEREMIAH JASON PAIGE

"So you know any more? Rosie heard anything? It's been days. Has the apartment been released? Is Pete staying there?"

"No, no, and no."

"But Rosie has been upfront and truthful with Pete. Right?"

"Yes. He's just not listening or he's listening and dismissing it or he is investigating Rosie's suspicions. That's all we know."

"Then, in the meantime, Rosie is full speed ahead."

"JJ, that's all she can do. This will help alleviate her feelings of guilt."

"What about the bottles? Are you all going to go through them?"

"Of course."

"You know all the information that Charles told about on the tape has to mean something."

"Yes, I agree but that's on the back burner as I finally got her to make a list."

"A list?"

"Yes, that's what we have done in the earlier matters. Sit down and just start throwing thoughts out there. Between the two of us bouncing what Rosie calls ideas and I call more theories, it seems to come to fruition."

"A list…"

"Yes, all I can say is it's worked in the past."

"Speaking of lists, I'm going to see about the horses and if the guys left anything on the board."

JAKE WILSON

"I understand, sir. I completely understand, and I by no means want to go back to prison. But JJ won't let me off the leash. I can't get that far into the property much less accomplish that."

"Yes, I know how to fly a drone. Hey, you're just paying me to watch the guy. You never said anything about my participation. Yes, he's telling the truth, JJ keeps him either tethered to the stables or the arena. And we both have been told in no uncertain terms we better never be caught near the house. What's the big deal about the waterfall? No sir, I apologize. By all means, sir. Yes sir."

THE SINCLAIR STABLES

JJ enters the stable through the east end portico. He grabs the clipboard and rips the sheet free. He turns and makes his way to the filly and Beauty glancing into each stall on the way. JJ stops and takes a step backward as something catches his eye through the open window. Was that lights at the far end of the east pasture?

ROSIE REDMOND ROSEMAN

"Connie, did you find it?"

"Yes, but I had to do some digging. I can't believe you didn't keep yours."

"I didn't say I didn't keep it. It's at the apartment, and remember my orders, I'm not to dare go there, especially after Pete settled down and started taking me seriously. I feel so much better knowing he has all his antennas up."

"We do too. Here."

"What's all this all over the paper? Curly ques and swirlies?"

"You could call them that. I call them doodles, mind relievers, you know. Soooo, my list might not be as complete as you think. I quite possibly could have let my mind wonder."

Rosie tosses Connie's doodled-up sheet back to her and grabs her notepad.

"Here read them to me."

"Excavated area by waterfall."

"Okay, we need to see that. JJ said he would take us."

"Yes, but that has been months ago."

"I know. Doesn't it just make you wonder what this land is hiding? What's next?"

"No oil lease."

"Yup. That's a biggie." Rosie jots, 'How rich do you have to be to say no to more money!' and then underlines.

"JJ ran off road and the car barely misses us."

"Dark blue SUV with GSW 24 something tag number."

Connie quips, "Or DSW."

"Remind me to ask JJ if the Sheriff's Office ever advised anything on those tag combinations? What's next?"

"That's all I've got."

"There was something else."

Rosie rises and walks to the French doors, and just as quickly turns.

"I'd better look in on Chris."

"No need. Madison has him down for his nap. I looked in when I snatched my notes."

"Let's take him to the stables when he wakes. I love it when he gets so excited to be on the horse, but then after he's up there he goes all quiet and stares to the side instead of looking forward."

Rosie grabs the pen from behind her ear and rushes to her pad.

"What is it? You just thought of something.

"Jake Wilson."

"What about him?"

Rosie writes, "Did they ever find Jake's girlfriend?"

"What's this?"

"It's the supply list I got from the stable hands."

"Why does it say dog food?"

JJ chuckles, "I added that. I wonder if there is a certain kind that dogs like better than others."

"I have no idea. Are we getting a dog?"

"Not exactly. We have a dog, or at least the ranch has a dog."

"Aah, who gave us a dog? Chris needs to see it. When can we go?"

"Woah. That's a lot of questions. Nobody gave us a dog he just kinda turned up, and before Chris gets all excited over him, I need to take him to the veterinarian and make sure he has his shots."

"Oh, good idea. Do you know what kind he is?"

"Yes, he's a Jack Russell Terrier. He's got loads of energy. I watched him fly through the air and snatch a bird right out of the sky. And the squirrels, he trees them so fast I about named him Flash."

"You've named him?"

JJ grins as he walks and shakes his head.

"Connie he is the cutest little thing. He is solid white with one brown ear and a brown patch. So I call him Patches and he already knows his name."

"Well, get that baby to the Vet, get all his shots, and flea medicine. Because I'm not going to be the reason Chris cries when he can't love on that dog."

THE ROCKING BAR P RANCH

"I feel guilty leaving Chris at the estate."

"He'll be fine. Madison dotes on him more than we do."

"I know she does, but that's not what I feel guilty over. You know how he loves to run everywhere out here. There's a lot less concrete and gravel here than at the estate."

"I have grass, you just have to get beyond the pool, stables, and garden."

"My exact point."

"Here comes JJ. Oh, now I feel guilty. Chris loves riding in the side by side. What's it called?"

"A Kawasaki Mule."

"He's got his little buddy with him."

"Get down Patches."

"No, leave him up there. Rosie and I will sit back here. How far is it to the waterfall?"

"A good jaunt. Hop in."

Connie and Rosie are laughing so hard, they're about to lose it. Patches' ears are flying straight out, and he even takes the bumps more gracefully than either of them.

"Don't have to worry about who is first off of here." Patches is out and gone chasing some unseen phenomenon.

"Where do we go from here, JJ?"

"Just up a little way, the waterfall is on your right."

"Very nice. Multiple levels. I wish we had come earlier. What a peaceful place."

The group turns at the sound of Patches' wild bark.

"What the heck?"

Everyone ducks as the spinning object nearly crashes into them, and just as quickly as it comes into focus, Patches flies into action, snatches it from the air, and with a yelp, swiftly releases it.

Connie grabs the pup and rapidly inspects his mouth as blood drips.

"Give me your handkerchief."

JJ checks his back pockets while he simultaneously stomps the apparatus into compliance.

JJ turns at a sound on the far side of the waterfall and starts in pursuit.

Rosie approaches in a stooped manner as if expecting further threat and/or danger from the now immobile object.

"What the bloody... Look how big that thing is."

JJ returns.

"Did you see anything?"

"No."

Rosie lowers her voice to an almost whisper. Her rapidity to process the situation promptly evaporates. Once again, Rosie's mind churns. She backs to what she considers a safe distance and motions to the others.

"Get over here."

Connie is not so quick to turn her back on the object that she feels is out of one's worst nightmare, even after JJ has stomped it into oblivion.

"What are you whispering for?"

"Shush. Don't you know those things can see, so what makes you think they can't hear?"

Rosie motions and walks further while she attempts to keep her voice in a lighter tone than anyone thought possible.

"I think…"

But her opinion will have to wait as thunder and lightning engulf the group and a mad dash ensues.

The ride back is fast and furious. Connie holds Patches as his previous seat is now occupied by the interloper, and Rosie makes one long hum sound while she concurrently taps her tooth with her fingernail.

MIKE DIXON

"I don't know what happened. I flew it to the exact coordinates of the waterfall, and as I was maneuvering it into position it disengaged. Were you able to get the information you wanted?"

THE ROCKING BAR P RANCH

The lodge kitchen is unusually congested, but eerily quiet. JJ lifts the drone from the stainless steel prep table as Rosie continues to shrewdly encroach upon the area.

With the pup at her feet, Connie is content to be a spectator. She brushes his head, which seems to be a silent command to happily yap while he engages in a burst of leaping and jumping, but another crack of thunder puts a quick end to all.

"What happened to the sweet summer rain?"

"It seems this monster that attacked us has brought the wrath of the gods with it."

"Hello, Boss?"

"I told you to quit calling me. I'll let you know if and when I need you."

"I understand, but..."

"Well, obviously you don't. What's so important today that wasn't this important the last time we talked? I told you to hang loose until the Judge gives us a go ahead for the Cease and Desist Order and that's when everything will have to come to a halt. Then we can let the Wilson boy do some spying for us."

"About that."

"What are you not telling me?"

"JJ, there is too much going on here, our apartment and then the lights in the east pasture at the estate, and now this drone at the ranch. All need to be investigated, but for now where are the girls?"

"Still in the kitchen."

"You need to move the girls out of there until we're certain no one is lingering and up to no good. You have a firearm?"

"A rifle but it's at the arena office."

"JJ, you have got to treat this situation as if there is someone there."

"Connie will go but…Pete, I'll let you talk to Rosie."

"No! I know Rosie will put up a fight but remind her she needs to see about Chris and that will help."

"This might not be the easiest thing to accomplish."

"Yup, why do you think I'm letting you do it?"

JAKE WILSON

"I refuse. I will not intentionally injure an animal."

"You little mealy mouth. One call and you'll be back in jail. Do you hear me?"

JEREMIAH JASON PAIGE

"Let's go."

"What did Pete say, is he coming?

Rosie closes in, still taking stock of the drone, but doesn't draw near.

"I bet this thing has some type of identifiable marks on it like the burner phones did."

"Come on, let's go."

Connie shoots a look JJ's way and JJ immediately knows bulldozing these two is not the answer, unless he wants another set-to with Connie. Rosie's a handful, but now Connie!

"Okay, Pete said to get out of here in case someone is still around and we are caught off guard. I don't mind it by myself, but not alone with the three of us, and besides, what about Chris."

That did it. Rosie is the first to lead the way.

JJ is close behind, as he thinks, *Pete, ole boy, you do know the magic words!*

"Get the wire cutters. Jake."

Jake turns but is frozen in place.

"Did you hear me? Get the wire cutters! I get hired to watch you, and this is what it gets me. I'm doing all the risky stuff and you do nothing."

"What are we doing?"

"I'm not into all that sadistic crap. I refuse to hurt the colt. I just agreed with him, but now we're cutting the fence and running the horses out."

"Not the filly and the colt. Mike just the Mustangs!"

"No, all of them. I don't know why this land is such a big deal but it must be worth a mint to go to all this trouble."

JAKE WILSON

"Connie, this is Jake and I haven't been upfront with you…"

"Hey punk, give me that phone."

CONSTANCE LOUISE SINCLAIR

"Oh J. We have to get home. That was Jake and something is wrong."

JJ steps on the gas.

"Charles is here."

Rosie says, "Bout time." As she looks upward.

"JJ, Charles didn't want you to go with Magic to California. He wanted you here and this is why, isn't it Charles."

Charles envelops the three occupants.

THE SINCLAIR ESTATES

"Rosie, get in the house, find Madison and Chris, lock the doors and set the alarm."

JJ grabs Connie by the arm. You're not coming. I don't know what I'm going to find in there. I can't think straight if I have you with me."

"I'm not leaving. He could be burning the stables down or even worse have the horses."

"Okay, stay close."

"JJ, Charles is here."

ROSIE REDMOND ROSEMAN

"Pete, where are you? Are you on the way? Do you know what's going on?"

"I'm on it. Are you safe? Are you with Chris?"

"Yes, yes."

"Stay put. Rosie, do you understand? Stay put!"

JEREMIAH JASON PAIGE

"Connie, grab some leads, the horses are out." Connie feels Charles, *Oh Charles, what is going on?*

"JJ, which way?" screams Connie, trying to be heard over the monstrous thunder and lightning. The rain pelts her from every direction.

"To the north. The fence is down!"

Connie struggles against the raging storm and sees JJ on the far side of the field with one horse in hand, but which horse? She pushes forward and pauses for a breath and sigh of relief. It's Beauty. She attaches the lead and passes one to JJ as he securely ties Beauty.

"We have to find the filly," JJ hollers. "She doesn't know her surroundings and might be lost forever. Let's head further this way, I bet they stayed together."

"I'll head back west."

"No Connie, stay with me. Connie!"

Connie fights through the pasture which is quickly becoming a bog. She shields her face as she turns further into the driving rain. Connie screams as she is pulled to the ground.

THE AFTERMATH

The ambulance moves forward with the only evidence of its presence strewn at Connie's feet. Rosie stands at the window with Chris safely in her arms. Connie shakes her head in a negative response. Rosie nods holds her son as tight as a mother can, and turns from the window as if to erase the happenings of the day. The worst of the storm has passed, or has it?

No, not for Geri and Ben. Connie felt some relief in being able to tell them their son had told her he could not compromise his principles even if it meant a return to prison, and he had taken a good beating for it.

JEREMIAH JASON PAIGE

The light of day does little to dispel what the group is feeling and Rosie is thankful Pete surrendered to her wishes and spent the night with his family.

"The Sheriff's Offices' Reserve deputies stood watch last night at the ranch. I'm determined to figure out what value that land could hold to drive a person or persons to this length. We know the horses were just a ruse to draw attention away from the area."

"Pete, when I heard her scream, and I thought I had lost her, it tore my guts out. You have no idea."

"JJ, you're talking like a man in love. You never know what you have until you think it is gone. Believe me on that one. We're going to get this figured out."

"I hope so, and soon."

"Let's see what the drone can tell us?"

THE LODGE

Pete removes his glasses. "It seems to me JJ, that you have effectively obliterated any identifiable serial numbers. The best we have is the make and model."

Rosie says, "I thought these were toys."

"Most are, but they are considerably smaller. I'm not certain, but if I were to make an educated guess, I'd say this one was large enough to be a transport drone. Deliver a pay-load for a company."

"I'd agree."

"JJ, when you gave pursuit through the woods, were you able to get close enough to make any type of identification?"

"No."

"Okay then, let's take a ride."

"Where to?

"The waterfall."

****

The mule coasts to a stop.

Pete with firm conviction, says, "You two stay put. JJ, point the way but let me have the lead."

"The pup is in pursuit of an unidentified hopping entity."

JJ feels no trepidation even with a sense of the unknown. Pete looks at JJ in a questioning aspect. JJ in a delayed response points forward and to the left.

The cracking of underbrush, the slow stalling manner of Pete, and the animated gestures of JJ, do not escape Connie and Rosie.

Rosie leans to stand up.

"What are you doing?"

"Walking down to the waterfall and take a look at the area again. "Pete said 'stay put'.""

"Connie, Connie, Connie, you are such a rule follower. Don't you get tired of having your mind occupied with fearful thoughts of retribution because you make a decision that you think is not in the rule book?"

"Okay, okay. What do you expect to find?"

"Everything, nothing. When we were here last time, my mind was busy looking over my shoulder so my mind didn't retain what my mind is pushing me to remember. My mind needs answers!"

Rosie stops, turns, and looks at Connie squarely. "I think we know why Charles wanted JJ to stay. I feel as if we have completely lost control and I'm a little overpowered by my feelings and being in these circumstances. I know, that's hard for you to believe. Thank heavens, though JJ stayed because I'm not nearly as fool-hearty as I was before Chris."

"Yes, I know you must worry about Pete, and now Chris, too."

"Pete, I wouldn't call worry. When I hear a siren or Pete is called in, I feel a comfort that he has been trained and is quite capable of doing his job, so I pray to God and ask Him to give Pete the knowledge the situation requires, and not to let him hesitate one second if he needs to pull his gun and fire."

Connie pats her friend.

At the waterfall, Connie sees a wild violet tenaciously anchored beside a tree root and thinks of her garden and Aunt Elsie's violets. Her serene remembrance is altered completely when a frog vacates its waterside post, and splashes unceremoniously belly first.

Rosie, with perfect calm and deportment, reclaims her personal space from Connie's attachment to her arm all resulting from her brief amphibian exposure. Rosie chuckles.

Connie says, "Sorry."

Connie accepts her enforced distance despite obvious discomfort.

Rosie scours the area once again then, suddenly a new emergence of knowledge wakes her mind. Rosie straightens. This ground has not only been dug up but has been leveled and collapsed back upon itself due to the rain."

The girls turn toward footsteps and holler, "Over here."

"I thought I told you to stay put." Pete thinks there's a fat chance of that.

"Did you find anything?"

"Yes, found where the grass and thick underbrush were trampled," replies Pete.

JJ says, "We followed as far as we could, and whoever it was got entangled in a wild blackberry patch."

"JJ, you know how you said the Driscolls have no idea what they are looking for?"

"Yes, the tape says it is some sort of an artesian well and this clearly isn't."

Pete inspects the area for the first time and gives a nod.

"Yes, exactly. So, what if they aren't looking to discover what the ground has hidden but are doing the hiding themselves."

Rosie turns to Connie. "There's a lot of unanswered questions on our pad, but this one is at the top of the list."

Pete says, "Let's get out of here. My gut is telling me to call Headquarters, and request the ground penetrating thermal imaging radar along with forensics."

Rosie eagerly encourages, "Then do it."

"No, if the results are, as I expect, we will be backed into a corner with no verifiable proof to support our allegations."

"What's your plan?"

"JJ, how fast and tight can you get this place locked down? I mean where it looks completely deserted."

"Quickly. Just say when."

"Now!"

CONSTANCE LOUISE SINCLAIR

Connie walks the length of the great room, arms crossed. She shakes her head as if to dispel the thoughts that so quickly are scrambled in her mind. She is cognizant of the question, but her sensibility leads to disbelief. Questions to understand or possibly glean some portents of the previous events.

"Connie, must I ask again, who is they? Did Jake say?"

"No, he has no idea, but he thinks it is the guy in the dark blue SUV. But it has to be Matthew Driscoll. I should have just given the land back."

"Too late for that thinking now. Besides, remember Charles."

JJ listens to the conversation and finds Rosie's mention of Charles' being in control does not send him into the continual battle with a ghost that he has spiraled into before. In the past, he felt defeated at the mention of Charles, because he had no idea how to fight for Connie with someone he can't feel, hear, see or touch.

"You all better turn in. Pete has this, and it's going to be a long night."

"Please, I want to see about Beauty."

"Let's all go." Rosie feels the need to stay together. Safety in numbers and all. *Thank you, Lord, for Madison and her family and for knowing Chris is safe with them on Banner Road. But Pete. Lord give him the quick ability to remember everything that he has been trained for in his moment of need, and bring him back safely to me. Amen*

Connie strokes Beauty. "I never thought I could feel this way about another horse as I have Magic. Magic was a gift from Charles, and even as a colt, he had great potential. Magic owned me and not me him from the moment he stepped off the transport. He spoke to my very being, my mind, body, and soul."

"And this pretty girl is not too shabby by any means."

"You're certainly correct there, Rosie. Her gray color glistens in the sun with flashes of deep purple undertones. Her short and stocky build makes her perfect for cutting and a great lead horse for Beauty."

"What's her name?"

"Officially, Greystone's Pewter Mist. Her Sire is Greystone and her Dam is Quicksilver's Mist, but her stable name is Misty."

"Oh, she likes me."

"Yes she does and what a long way you have come, my friend. Remember your fears of being around Magic. Look at you letting her put her head over your shoulder. Rub her muzzle."

"No, that's okay. I'm good for now."

"We're going to have you in the saddle before long and Chris, too. JJ, let's find a pony for Chris!"

Rosie's smile would impress even the Cheshire cat.

"JJ, I have news."

"Wait Pete, I'm being inundated from all sides."

"Should I ask who from? If it's the girls, go ahead and put me on speaker."

Rosie clamors to be the first to speak.

"Pete, did you get any sleep? You good?"

"Yes sweetheart, I'm good. How about you all?"

"We're good too. What did you find out? Catch them red-handed? Have you requested the radar stuff?"

"I wish, but no. No activity, not even a drive by. But the Sheriff's Office got Mike Dixon in custody and he's spilling his guts. Scared to death, but more scared of going to jail than his employer, or I should say his second employer."

"That's good. So did they confiscate his cell phone and does the number match the number in Jake's phone and who is doing this OKCPD or Canadian County Sheriff's Office?"

"Woah, slow down."

"Oh."

"OKCPD has Jake's phone, but Mike's phone is with the Sheriff. I am certain that they are coordinating though but more certain it's a burner so unless we get lucky and have a video might be a dead end."

"And the SUV, nothing on it?"

"It was found and had been reported stolen."

"Any fingerprints?"

"No, wiped clean. I need to go. I have to meet with the DA on possible charges. Not looking good, usually trespassing is our last resort but how do you make that stick when they are your employees?"

JAKE WILSON

"Connie, this is Jake."

"Jake, please address me as Mrs. Sinclair, as only my friends and I are on first name basis."

"Sorry, yes, I'm so sorry for everything. I just wanted out of prison and I jumped at the opportunity."

"Jake, this is JJ as Mrs. Sinclair is in turmoil over the events that got us to this point, and she feels you have betrayed her."

"Jake, how could you? We have been neighbors your entire life. We have looked to each other's needs, and that is why I didn't have a qualm about helping out, because, you know what Jake, that's what neighbors do. When I found you in the east pasture, I almost didn't recognize you until you said my name. You were at death's door."

"I understand, can you ever forgive me?"

"Yes of course, as long as you truly comprehend the gravity of your actions. And the horses, to be released during a storm this close to the highway, what horrible results that could have had."

"I know, but that is when I tried to stop Mike. They asked me to maim the colt, and I refused, and then Mike refused and he decided to cut the fence."

"So that's when he attacked you?"

"That's when we fought and I lost as he had the advantage with the wire cutters."

Connie feels herself becoming calm.

"How are you? You sound much better, and I want you to know that you must be hurting over Keri's death. I know that the loss of her life has to have had an impact on you."

"Thank you, Connie. Mother said you called quite often to inquire and…"

"Yes, go ahead, Jake."

"I want to thank you for what you have done for me."

"Jake, you have a lot to overcome. Your parents have worked most of their life building a home for you and your brother. The Wilson name is said with respect. Do you understand, your name, Jake Wilson, is all you have and the Wilson name tells who you are. When it is spoken, people have an immediate reaction. Good or bad. Jake, people's response to the Wilson name is up to you. Do you understand?"

"Did the drone do the job?"

"Yes and all is good. The rain did me a favor. It pinpointed the exact location."

"So they are no wiser to the situation. I can't believe you used my property."

"Well, at the time, it wasn't your property and still isn't, so I thought I would drop this in Sinclair's lap. Remember, you said to handle it."

"So, what's the holdup?"

"Shouldn't be much longer, I diverted their attention to the Sinclair woman's house to keep them from doing more snooping. It seemed to have worked but I want to give it a day or so then I can get in there and get everything handled."

"Where's the other girl, Keri's friend? She should be asking questions by now." After a pause in the conversation. "Never mind, I don't want to know and remember Kirby, same deal as California. DAK."

THE ROCKING BAR P RANCH

The third night of stakeout. Pete settles in. Pete looks to the west wishing the sun was down. They are an hour into it and on radio silence. Pete looks around the area and sees no one, which is exactly the plan. Pete shifts uncomfortably and knows from previous surveillances that it will be well after midnight if then, before any action.

Pete is beginning to question his thinking about pushing for an additional night. No, the drone was sent for a reason and both Jake and Mike had been instructed to check for any disturbance west and north of the waterfall. The guy is gonna show.

Danny has two units positioned where Evans Road dead ends into Memorial Road.

Pete stiffens. A car passes going east on Memorial Road but never slows. Danny and Pete have taken a chance that the front entrance on Hefner will not be used due to the surveillance system, which is noted on signage.

At the estate, Pete knows JJ, Connie and Rosie are diligently going through the contents of the milk jugs perchance surveillance is a bust, and the answers the jars hold could put this whole investigation to bed. Pete knows Danny had to use every weapon in his arsenal to talk his Captain into extending more money and resources.

Pete stretches and wishes he had taken Rosie's advice and laid down instead of napping in the recliner. He reaches for coffee just as his radio keys one time, the signal for entry to the property through the back entrance.

Pete starts to rise for a better look as the sun has not fully set. Then a transmission comes in a low whisper, "One on foot."

KIRBY KERMAN

Kirby is no stranger to stealth missions. After serving with the Seals, and deployment to countries under the guise of tourists on safari this was a cakewalk. Navy protocol dictated advancing after midnight, closer to two to five in the morning, geared up with camo face and hand black.

Kirby had thought of forgoing the Navy's total black mandate, but as always, it gave him the stellar feeling of accomplishment, and, well, old habits are hard to break.

Kirby would have waited the extra time, but he knew he was at a disadvantage because the last time he had made a trip to the waterfall was by the front entrance on Hefner. Now coming off Memorial Road, he needed every benefit the meager twilight could offer. And even in years prior, he barely got the job accomplished, and that was only after locking those two women in the cellar. He wouldn't mind taking them out.

As he made his way, Kirby thought of his brother still serving their country, and his father's company doing federal contracts for the government, not to mention his uncle. Kirby knew they sensed his mercenary tendencies, but knew they didn't fault him for it.

Kirby looked back to keep himself oriented. This was just a recon mission and he would return the way he came after verification the end goal was obtainable.

But then…Kirby drops to the ground and belly crawls out of sight. With labored breathing, he places his hand on his gun and presses his back to the tree. He strains to see in the now darkened surroundings. His training and instincts, always dead on, brought this ominous feeling that he knows not to ignore. What was it he heard?

He changes locations in the direction of what he can only hope is the lodge as he realizes what he had heard was actually what he was not hearing. The cicadas had gone silent.

OKLAHOMA CITY POLICE DEPARTMENT

Pete is bone tired, but not because of the three straight nights of heightened anticipation. Pure dejection was what was kicking his butt.

Pete paces the all too familiar area in front of Danny's desk as they wait for the inevitable call from the Captain's office. Dispatch had told them, over the air and not by mobile, to 10-19 the Captain's office. What a slap in the face, everyone was instantly made aware.

"Pete, come on, settle down. We may have lost the battle but CSI is out there with digital imaging. They still can find something."

"But, I wanted to catch him in the act. If I hadn't promised, if only the department would okay an additional night we'd have an assailant, I wouldn't feel so bad."

"Pete, remember you weren't in with the Captain on your own, I was pledged to this mission right along with you."

"What's taking so long? Let's get in there and get this over."

ROSIE REDMOND ROSEMAN

"Twenty-seven jars and with only three jars left we find the sweet, sweet answer. Connie read it again. It is almost like hearing angel's voices."

"You are so funny Rosie, but I'm right there with you. At last, we have verification of everything Charles has been leading us toward, but how will this help Pete and Danny?"

"We should have gone and not let JJ deter us. He had so many reasons why he should go alone that by the time my mind had come up with all the answers, he was gone."

"I know, but he can do it faster and he left us things to do. Call OSU Extension Office, Oklahoma Water Resources Board, and Oklahoma Division of the EPA."

"But we are the ones that know the exact part of the basement the thingy should be located. What was it called?"

"A buttress."

"And what else?"

"You're trying to get me mixed up so I'll read it again."

"No."

"It said wellhead enclosed in a concrete buttress located in the southeast corner of the lodge basement."

"And the tape was right. Charles' Uncle Cecil from Lawton wished the well and the same Uncle Cecil called it a once in a lifetime find. A sweet well. Whatever that means."

KIRBY KERMAN

"Hey Boss, transfer money to me. I've gotta lie low. It was a setup. I got out okay but had to abort the mission. Do you understand?"

"Yes Kirby, get out of town until I get this figured out."

"No problem there."

Matthew Driscoll leans into his overstuffed office chair and repeatedly rubs the smooth leather as he contemplates the time remaining before he receives a knock on the door. Time to cover his bases.

OFFICE OF DETECTIVE DANIEL DOBBIN'S
OKLAHOMA CITY POLICE DEPARTMENT

"Yeah, he's here. I'll tell him. Yes, he will be glad to know."

During Danny's phone conversation, Pete has ceased his pacing and has leaned, with both his arms extended, dead center on Danny's desk. Pete's tie hovers precariously over Danny's nameplate.

Danny looks up and retreats further into his chair.

"That was Nick, CSI liaison. The imaging is complete and they have located two anomalies. Cadaver dogs are on the scene along with forensics and backhoes dispatched."

FLAGG AND FLAGG LAW OFFICE

"Mrs. Sinclair, this is Lynda with Flagg and Flagg Law Firm, and Richard wanted me to tell you that Driscoll's have filed a motion quashing their court action and there will be no Cease and Desist order forthcoming."

Connie feels Charles. *Hello baby!*

CAPTAIN'S OFFICE
OKLAHOMA CITY POLICE
DEPARTMENT

"Come in, gentlemen. Job well down. Because of you, two families, who have been looking for years, can lay their daughters to rest, and the Chief would like the two of you to be on the podium during the news conference."

ROSIE REDMOND ROSEMAN

"It's good to be home. Home sweet home. There's no place like home."

"Rosie, enough, before I start singing 'Oh Home on the Range.'"

"Pete, watch out or he's gonna get your shin with his trike, again."

"Come here you little rascal."

Pete walks the short distance to the apartment door, down the sagging chipped concrete steps, and places his son on the small patch of grass.

Rosie leans in the doorway with her hands in her apron pockets, as she watches Pete introduce the intricate working of a rolly polly to Chris. Pete looks up and smiles. Rosie thanks the Lord for these two loves of her life.

"Connie, come to the great room."

"What's up?"

JJ lifts Connie.

"Connie, we have been through so much. All the ups and down, all the financial disasters. What would it be like to have all our dreams come true? I've often wondered how things in my life somehow turn out topsy-turvy, but this time topsy-turvy may have landed right side up."

JJ saunters to the fireplace with a grand smile as he continues shaking his head in disbelief.

"We were thinking the lodge well was a sweet well and on the level of an artesian."

"Yes."

"Well, look at this."

Connie takes the letter and sits on the arm of the leather couch. JJ walks the length of the fireplace and back again. His anticipation builds.

Connie glances back to the letterhead.

"Oklahoma State University."

"Yes, the water I left at the OSU Extension Office was sent to Oklahoma State University for analysis."

"I see that, but it doesn't mention anything about the sweet well."

"No, but it mentions traces of rare metal."

ROSIE REDMOND ROSEMAN

"You're home? How was it?"

"Wonderful. JJ and I both wish you could have gone. We haven't had any couples time forever."

"But, when you have a toddler you can't just jump and go. I've never been to Vegas but Pete has. He said a group of friends use to do a three-day junket twice a year."

"We didn't do a lot of casinos. JJ isn't much of a gambler, hates to watch his money disappear into the machine."

"I can understand that."

"We stayed at the Mirage. Went right to the restaurant after we unpacked and they seated us at an oval booth surrounded by a saltwater aquarium. It was still early for their dinner menu, but somehow the waiter took control and started us off with champagne over lemon ice. Cooled us down quickly. Then they brought a cup of vichyssoise."

"Hate to interrupt but a cup of what?"

"Cold potato leek soup."

"Oh."

"Don't feel bad the only reason I knew was as the waiter placed our food he whispered, 'potato soup'. I googled for the leek part."

Rosie laughs, "Well that makes me feel better. What was the main course?"

"JJ got prime rib, of course. I had lobster and it came out as a work of art. There was no shell and huge claws, all swimming in a creamy butter sauce."

"I like it when someone else does all the work. And the horse show."

"Let me correct you there. The Run for a Million is far from a horse show. This is the culmination of not only a year's work but a lifetime of preparation. The horses are trained daily at a trainer's facility to keep them in peak condition. A few weeks before each event, which comes in close succession, the horsemen and trainers tune the horses up on whatever element they seem to be apprehensive upon."

"So did she win?"

"You mean Calla, Calla Leck?"

"Yes."

"No, unfortunately. She dropped a rein, but Buddy was spectacular. What a horse."

"Oh no. I'm sorry."

"No need to be because what a run she has had to be thirteen and in the saddle for only a year and make it through NRHYA, then first in the World in OKC and the big event. The Run for a Million. We all will be keeping her in our prayers and anxiously watching her participate in all the upcoming events."

"Rosie in a softened voice and a heavy sigh, says, "That child must have been born with this purpose in mind."

"I think she was. She's a twin and her parents put great thought into each child's name, and in this case, the child found her calling. You know what JJ said?"

"What."

"Don't you love it when your life has a purpose, and you can see the marked road before you and the reason you were born."

ROSIE REDMOND ROSEMAN

Rosie paces the lodge porch. Connie sits on the top step. JJ is on the phone. Each person is lost in thought or on a mission. Their short break from prepping for the grand opening seems to have been extended by some revelation.

JJ says, "Great, thanks."

"What, tell us?"

Connie stands, "I know that was the OSU geophysicist."

"Yes, it has been confirmed. The land contains rare minerals that will be used in bio conductors, cars, our phones, and, get this, there's even a chance in a Space X rocket."

"That's great and…"

JJ leans his shoulder into the substantial lodge doors. "Connie we'll talk later. I have to make some more calls, and probably see about making these doors handicap…"

Connie turns to Rosie as Rosie continues pacing but this time stops at the far north end of the expansive porch.

Connie walks and seats herself on the arm of the chair. One of many.

"Isn't that wonderful?"

"You'd think, wouldn't you?" Rosie turns, arms entwined.

Connie slides into the chair. Rosie joins her. The friends rock.

"Connie, you understand what you have done. JJ is set to become a very rich man."

"JJ is it still going good."

"Huh?"

"You and Connie. Amanda talked to Connie the other day about the colt and she didn't find out anything. So you and Connie are good or was your rendezvous a failure."

"About that!"

AMANDA BORDILLON HARTLY

Amanda enters the stables while lifting her shiny black hair off her neck. The heat is crushing today. She pulls her tresses up in a ponytail that she secures with a hair tie which seems to inevitably be attached as a bracelet on her wrist, then with a double twist, it is all secured with a claw clip atop her head.

Miguel, along with José and Flipé seems to be transitioning well into their supervisory positions and are busy deploying the ranch hands to their respective duties.

José moves his hat to his chest and offers, "Señorita, am I to saddle your horse?"

"Yes please, and do you know which direction Señor Hartly rode?"

The cadence of the horse brought back memories from Amanda's appearances at youth events where she competed in Ranch Trail, Showmanship, and Western Pleasure. Amanda blushes remembering the compulsory attire she wore. If you were in those events you did not worry about thunder thighs because your leg movements told your mount what was expected of him. A competitor's friend said as she watched Amanda back her horse around a corner without dislodging a pole that it was like jackknifing a semi.

Amanda stops her horse to see if all horses have the quality of motion her show horse displayed. She relaxes the reins and the pony starts to walk. Amanda reins him in and this time upon relaxing the reins he doesn't offer any movement. She presses her knee followed by the heel of her boot and he moves counter clockwise. She straightens him and repeats the procedure with an added opposing knee and he sides steps using his entire body. Amanda leans forward and gives him sturdy pats on his neck.

"Good boy, with a little work. But, for now, that wasn't too bad."

"Hey, you looking for me? I just saw your text. What's up? And what were you doing?"

"Oh, I'm embarrassed you saw that. Just having a déja vu moment, but tell me what did JJ say? Was there romantic alone-time enough to send them forward, or are they still stuck? I want them to have what we have. A solid, stable relationship upon which to build."

"JJ said when he went to bed in the wee hours of the morning everything had been reestablished, but he awoke a couple of hours later and saw the outside security lights on."

"Oh no, she had left?"

"No, not that drastic. Connie is used to permanence, a feeling of security that, I'm afraid my dear, your uncle has not mastered. You know Amanda, there is not that much difference in your ages but I'm telling you that you are more mature than JJ."

"Doug, that's not fair. JJ has been struggling to try to play catch up ever since he liquidated and bought half of Magic. Now, we have Magic and the ranch AND the trust Charlie set up for me. Tell me what JJ has. Just tell me!"

ROSIE REDMOND ROSEMAN

"Come in. That was a quick trip into the city."

"Not really. I was on my way when I called," Connie says in a muted manner.

"No need to whisper, even if Chris is asleep, nothing wakes that child. Sit down, what did you want to talk about?"

Connie sits on the sofa but looks straight past the TV and out the window. Connie turns, strokes her throat, pulls a leg under her, and pushes back into the corner of the coach.

"Oh, Rosie. Tell me what to do. Which way do I turn?"

"You in a rocky patch again."

"Not right now, all seems good."

"I swear you two. What's it gonna take to smooth this road you're on."

"I don't know, I don't know!"

Rosie shifts and mirrors Connie's position on the sofa, as she ponders Connie's last admission.

"Seems like this is a broken record. Never knowing which way to turn. How many times must we have this conversation?

Remember I told you in the car at the lodge that you two can't be on the same page at the same time talking about it and agreeing on how good things should be.

You need to talk about what is acceptable and expected in your relationship. You are comfortable when JJ is uncomfortable, and when JJ is comfortable you are uncomfortable, and you don't know how to handle it."

Connie shifts her position feeling the temperature rise in her body.

"Rosie, you're right sometimes it seems as if we don't even know each other."

"Because you don't talk, and…"

"No, we talk. I have told him my entire life or…"

"Or what? Now we're getting to it. Spit it out. Come on!"

"He knows about everything from the beginning with Charles and I, but…"

"But what? That you know nothing about him."

"And maybe that's the first truthful statement you have made about this entire relationship. Does your life have to be in conflict and JJ on a white horse for this to work?"

Connie stands as she takes offense.

"Really Rosie," Connie states in a slurred drawn out tone.

"JJ on a white horse. I've done the same for him, trying to make a way for him to feel secure. A life with a purpose."

"Is that what you call it? A purposeful life. You're good if you are doing for someone else, having engagement parties, and the such. But what do you know, really know about JJ and him about you?"

Connie turns her back.

Rosie stands.

"You came here and ask me what to do, but you always ask without really wanting to know."

"Oh, yes I do."

"Okay then, we'll just see about that. You want to know, full truth with no hold backs?

Connie turns and sees Rosie's dogged manner to pursue this to the end. Connie cringes.

"Connie, dern your hide. Have you ever needed anything in your life? Have you held a job just to keep yourself above water and a roof over your head?"

Connie diverts her eyes from Rosie. She feels an unanticipated shock along with a startling coldness that hits her at her core.

Rosie stands, eye to eye with Connie, and knows she came for one thing and one thing only, to have Rosie bolster her feelings, to find vindication in Rosie as Rosie always seems to agree, but not this time.

"Connie, I have listened and listened and listened. I have bitten my tongue. You two seem to be children in a sandbox each taking turns at destroying each other's creation or destroying even the partial attempt at creating something. What's wrong with you? Do you even know what you want?

Connie reaches for a Kleenex.

"No Ma'am, don't you even start with those tears. You just want me to condone and even reinforce your bad behavior that ends in a hug fest?"

Rosie tries to walk, but the apartment's limitations suddenly feel confining.

"Remember, you asked, so let's make a list. Yes, why not, wasn't that your idea just a short few days ago?"

Connie feels a flush of adrenaline mingling with her thoughts and disorientation tingling through her body.

"You want, Charles gets. A horse, a house, a Lexus, clothes, and not cheap clothes, designer clothes, jewels, paintings, party upon party. Am I close, can you deny one word so far?"

Connie's embarrassment is hindering her ability to think. To come up with any plausible defense. She wants to cry but she dares not as she seems to feel some perceived fright with Rosie's threatening tone.

Connie straightens. No, Connie will not succumb to her first impulse. She will not let Rosie see her cry.

"Okay, let's look at JJ's list. JJ, lost everything when he sold out to try and rescue you from the mess Charles left you in. No offense, Charles."

Connie flinches as she tries to pull together some reasoning to counter Rosie's thought process but swiftly switches gears as she thinks Rosie sure isn't offending Charles, even apologizing to him.

"Then he bought half of Magic and gave that to you. Every penny he had went to let you know that he cherished you to the point of bankrupting himself. Now that's gone as a gift to the kids."

"Do you see my point?

Rosie quickly continues leaving her rhetorical question hanging. No matter where JJ stands you don't know how to handle it. And guess what all of that is too late because now the bucks are rolling in, and just maybe JJ is in the driver's seat."

Rosie stops only for emphasis, but then...

Pete stands aghast.

CONSTANCE LOUISE SINCLAIR

Connie forcefully shuts the car door but doesn't attempt to start the car. Right now, Connie wants to be alone. She nods to dislodge the defeatist thoughts scrambling about. Connie looks for Kleenex. Where are they? She looks to the passenger side floorboard and is startled to find the box in easy reach.

She feels the cold feeling of weariness even as the heat whelms around her. She blots her watering eyes that is a small reflection of her inward thoughts but doesn't give way. Connie feels her usual response to take flight, and flee any uncomfortable situation, instead she whispers a calming promise, if only, as she winces. Connie knows she can easily obsess over the hurtful words. She will not live with this negativity. She cannot embrace dread and hopelessness.

Connie slams the box into the dashboard.

ROSIE REDMOND ROSEMAN

Rosie dials as she moves like one of Chris' windup toys caught in a loop.

"JJ, Connie ask for my opinion of your relationship and dern it, I told her. No, she left, I don't know where."

"Pete, give me the car keys, Chris is asleep and a snack will tide him over until I get back."

"No."

"What do you mean no?"

"No. Not until you sit down and no, not until you calm down."

Rosie, with arms akimbo, paces as the room's small dimensions are further compacted with each breath.

JEREMIAH JASON PAIGE

"Connie, Rosie called and she's sorry."

The phone goes dead. JJ pulls his Rubicon off the road and redials. Voicemail.

"That bad, huh."

JJ opens his app and sees Connie is headed west on NW Highway. He flips his Jeep around on Hefner Road and turns North on Evans. The six miles north to the estate seems forever. His mind races as he logically thinks through every reasonable scenario.

CONSTANCE LOUISE SINCLAIR

Connie is livid, much to her consternation, as she continues to digest, process, and relive Rosie's revelation. Her situation only contributes to her anxiety and clouds her judgment.

She retreats to her penchant to run from problems. But not today.

What to do! Where to go!

She thinks of Magic and the release she receives while she clings tightly as Magic responds with his power leaving her unfortunate circumstances behind.

JEREMIAH JASON PAIGE

JJ drives through the west entrance gates, but no Lexus. He continues out the drive and speeds toward the north gate. No car.

JJ enters the house, hears the alarm still engaged, then heads for the south end of the stables. He sees Connie's car.

JJ enters the barn, and heads north stepping in every stall as he advances. Nothing. He passes the unlocked tack room and continues north. But why would she park at the south end if she is going to ride, and without changing to her boots.

Memories flash lightning fast to the other time he had lost Connie during the rain. Fear had possessed him then, fear possesses him now.

JJ turns to view the area and realizes all the Mules are at the ranch. The filly it is.

CONSTANCE LOUISE SINCLAIR

Connie leans back and lets Beauty withdraw from a full gallop. Connie is pleasantly surprised that her planned attempt to regain control through a full-out cry, did not occur. Not even a snivel and the crushed Kleenex box was the real loser.

So, Rosie is right. Crying has been my defense against anything I can't control. She bristles as she swears that ugly crying would never be acceptable to her again. No one can make me cry. No one will hold that power. No. Connie may never cry again.

And, do JJ and I know each other, or do I look for some ruse to use as a type of glue to sustain us? Do I like to see him comfortable, purposeful, and fulfilled or do I regale in his struggles?

Connie stops at the crest of the hill to grasp the rare opportunity of seeing the glistening pond wind free.

Connie dismounts and takes a moment to praise Beauty then walks down to the patch of boulders she has used for years as her ride destination.

The lacebark elms, as always, offer shade but in this windless moment, she misses their shimmer.

Connie bends to identify a praying mantis moving on the violet petals of the Echinacea.

"What are you praying about my friend? Whatever it is could you add my name? Thanks, I appreciate it."

Connie picks a pink buttercup which is copious in the pasture. I will leave you alone out here, but not in my garden.

The warmth of the rock, along with the sun, hug her like old friends.

Connie circumspectly ponders while she quantifies her decision to ask for Rosie's help. She accepts the truths Rosie put forth, but the vigor of her presentation may be suspect. Either way that does nothing to mitigate the feeling of being stripped naked without a blade of grass under which to retreat.

Connie releases any hard feelings because that's what friends do, they call each other out on bad behavior. And Rosie did just short of saying, stop it, stop it right now.

Connie hears the canter of the filly and sees JJ's tall angular frame cast into shadow.

"Rosie it can't possibly be that bad. JJ will find her."

"No Pete, it was bad. I went too far. I just stopped short of calling her a spoiled brat."

"You didn't though did you?"

"No, but by my surmising, it could be taken that way."

"Well, you don't know for certain she accepted your words with the full weight you seem to believe. So let's hold on to that, for now."

JEREMIAH JASON PAIGE

"Is this seat taken?" Comes from a warm and caring voice.

Connie looks up with a smile. She accepts the feeling that always brings pleasure upon seeing him. Connie focuses on JJ's tousled hair and thinks that is one of his many desirable qualities.

"Not if you don't mind sitting with someone that has just had a good comeuppance as Rosie would say."

Connie glances away pretending a brief interest in the grass by her knee.

"I gathered as much. Rosie is distraught."

"Well good. No, I don't mean that. I ask her and she told."

"I gathered that, also."

JJ is reluctant to continue because he doesn't know what opinion Rosie gave to Connie about their relationship. And he was glad he wasn't privy to the conversation at all. But, whatever side Rosie took he just prayed it left him with a shred of dignity and a lot of hope.

"Do you know what Rosie thinks?" Connie asks with an exaggerated quality.

"No." JJ at this moment is questioning his judgment but stands firm while he awaits the outcome. Calm and cool, calm and cool is his mantra.

"She thinks we don't know each other. That we never talk. That we have never sat down and had a long lengthy all-encompassing talk without being in crisis or close to it."

JJ feels stress peppered with a trace of fear, but if this will end, once and for all, their strained relationship, he must push forward.

"What do you want to know?"

"Tell me about your family."

"Connie, you know about Amanda and Margaret."

"No silly, your grandparents, your mother, and dad, where were you raised."

"Right. I was born in Bakersfield. My parents were older when I was born as Margaret and I have different dads. There were thirteen years between Margaret and me so that's why Amanda and I are so close in age."

"Your mother was divorced then?"

"No, Margaret's dad took his own life and mother thought she would never remarry. The story goes, from the time my dad first saw mother, he couldn't take his eyes off her. He owned the construction company that had the contract on a complete remodel of a neighbor's house. Dad…"

"What was his name?"

"Oh. But of course, James Jason Paige."

"Why am I not surprised."

JJ shifts to the ground but never losses Connie's gaze.

"Jason has been passed down and used in every son's name, I guess for generations."

"That will truly build valor into a family especially if honor and integrity are associated with it."

"Funny you should say that. I have always been told it means, loyal warrior."

Connie thinks, well you've lived up to that then. As JJ continues, Connie feels a new ease being born between them.

"Construction? You worked for your father?"

"Yes and my uncle. Uncle Carl. A master at cabinetry."

"No wonder the ranch has gained such a reputation in such a short amount of time, construction is in your blood."

"Yes, I guess it is."

"How long were you there?"

"I inherited my father's half of the company, an endeavor I didn't take lightly. Big shoes to fill, and all."

Connie shutters as she loses focus turns solemn, and tenses.

"Connie are you okay? Connie."

Connie clutches her hand to her chest as she feels her breath escape her as she nods her reply. Her heart aches. She smiles but cannot keep a slight quiver from appearing. She has to ask even though she knows the answer.

"And now?"

"And now?"

"Yes, the company's ownership?"

"Connie, you have to understand when I became owner that was the most important thing in my life. You know, to continue. I thought of it as a legacy. But now…"

"J, you did that for me."

"I use to think of it that way but not anymore, Connie. When I approached Uncle Carl, he understood completely. He hugged me and said, 'Son, go rescue your girl.'"

JJ turns and faces the pond, places his hands behind his head, and speaks with a calm peacefulness, devoid of any remorse.

"It's a vague memory. Because here we are today. With this great life. The kids settled. The ranch and the grand opening."

"Why did I not know this? JJ, how could I not know?"

JJ shrugs. "I guess you never ask."

"That woman."

"Who?"

"Rosie, Rosie was right."

"That doesn't matter whose right."

JJ, now beside her, says, "No backward thoughts, only forward, upward, even skyward."

"Oh J, why are we always caught up in something."

"Babe, it's not like it's of our own doing."

JJ grabs Connie's hand to not only hold it. But to intertwine fingers in hopeful expectation of the inexhaustible feelings of love and devotion that he has now come to find so comforting, settling, and irreplaceable.

"You remember when you ask me if we are good? If our relationship could withstand the turbulence that Pete and Rosie's marriage came through. Do you Connie?"

"Yes."

"Do you remember what my answer was?"

"Yes, you said, 'time will tell.'"

"Connie, look at me."

Connie turns with her head cowered. Connie forces a smile until she looks into those smoky deep brown eyes. The peace she sees in him is unexplainable, unfathomable. He gave up so much, and for me, but even after everything, the satisfaction she sees in him acknowledges their future to come, while erasing the past.

"This is our time, Connie. Yes, time has told us this is our moment, the beginning of our lives."

ROSIE REDMOND ROSEMAN

"Pete, its Connie!"

"Well, answer it."

"Oh Connie, are you alright? We came looking, but couldn't find you two anywhere. I'm so sorry. Can you ever forgive me? I didn't mean those things I said. I need to see you. Where are you? I'm coming."

Nothing but silence.

"Connie, I completely understand if you never want to talk to me again. Connie?"

Rosie moves her phone and stares into it as if some new technology was going to emit invisible answers to every one of her questions.

Snickers erupt.

"Oh Rosie, I just can't let you off the hook that easy. JJ and I couldn't. Well, at least, I couldn't resist a moment of torment."

"Then you're okay. We're okay. Are we still friends."

"Yes, we're still friends, and because of that push you gave me. Well, I want to tell you about the talk that resulted from it. I bet you didn't know JJ was quite the bronc rider in his younger day."

Connie reaches for JJ's hand contemplating the talks yet to come.

JEREMIAH JASON PAIGE

"Hello Connie, I'm on my way."

"Seriously, we are doing this?"

"I'm not anything if I'm not a man of my word. Go change, then meet me in the stables. I've called and the ranch hands should have Beauty ready."

"No need to change, I have been sitting, waiting in anticipation of our ride. And you promised we can do this more often, right."

"Yes, we've got horses and I've turned the rest of the arena and Lodge over to Hoyt Bower. He will do us a good job. His references had high praise for him."

"They saddling the filly for you. No, I'm hauling the Chestnut stallion you got me for our ride."

"I am so glad you like him. I know he wasn't the reason we went to the horse and stallion sale, but I could tell you were hooked."

"He was hard to say no to."

"And now, you don't." Connie giggles in that way that reinforces JJ's sentiments.

AMANDA AND DOUGLAS HARTLY

"Good news. No delays. We're getting ready to board. You all are going to pick us up at the airport. Landing at noon."

"Yes, I'm on my way to go for a ride with Connie, then we will come to get you, and later tonight I have reservations at Fait Maison in Edmond. Pete and Rosie are meeting us there. Connie has no idea, but I think we can pass it off as a celebration of all of us being together and a pre-event celebration of the Ranch opening."

Amanda is giddy. "I won't be able to stand it. To be there when you do this is wonderful. I know you have put a lot of planning into this to make it extra special."

"Sis, you need to hold the vibration decibel to at least a two and no higher. You hear me. Then after the restaurant scream and cry all you want."

THE BOULDERS

"Could life get much better than this?"

"Seems impossible doesn't it."

"Connie, you are happy, right."

"Yes, immeasurably. Oh J, don't you feel it, the comfort between us. We know each other, and that is no small thing."

"Connie, everything is falling into place. I can be the man I need to be. I'm at the place I was when I took over Dad's construction company. Self-sufficient, in my realm of knowledge. Connie I can take care of us. On my own with you never having to worry about anything. I'm there."

"I'm there too. You are my forever and always. I will walk beside you no matter what life brings."

"Babe, you know how I know this is our time?"

Connie scoots closer and runs her arm into his. They grasp hands. "Tell me."

"I know it's our time because there is a peace within me, within my heart that will always be there."

Connie lays her head on his shoulder and says, "Can we stay here forever, in this one perfect moment? This moment when all is right."

"I know everyone will be upset with me as this ruins the grand affair tonight, but..."

JJ checks his pocket, and drops to one knee.

"Connie, this was my mother's ring and it is a one of a kind as she and dad designed it at Treasures, Inc. My mother was very dear to me as you are. Connie, I can finally say, let me take care of you. Connie if you will have me, will you be my wife."

PETER ROSEMAN

"Rosie, you better get a move on if we're going to drop Chris by Madison's house."

Pete stops in the middle of placing toys in Chris' diaper bag as he is startled to hear heels coming down the hall. Rosie in high heels? He picks Chris up and walks to the front room entry as Rosie turns the corner.

Pete is speechless. Rosie stands in an emerald green tea-length spaghetti strap dress. Her red hair is caught up with a green velvet ribbon making her eyes manifest in a most becoming way.

"What? I told you I got a new dress. Hey, Pete! Hello, I need your help with this neckless. Pete, give me Chris and help me."

Pete bends to place Chris on the floor.

Rosie says, "Give him to me, so he stays clean."

Pete says, "Not a chance. You look perfect and you're staying perfect."

THE GRAND OPENING

Valet, upon valet dash to accommodate the cars entering the three lane drive. Every dress style is seen and some men's attire, which seems to match that guest's personality perfectly, appears from straight-up cowboy to formalwear.

The guest list rivals the beginning days at the Sinclair estate and even in some ways challenges its authenticity. Of course, there is Joyce and Phillip Chapman of Enid, the Northrups of Ponca, Lynda and Richard Flagg of El Reno along with the Governor of Oklahoma and his wife, who doesn't make many events, and Oklahoma Senators, and state representatives.

We are exceedingly honored to be able to entertain the Mayor of El Reno, Matt Whiten, and his lovely wife Elisha. Matt has worked tirelessly to generate the workers, not only for construction but stable hands to keep up with the everyday riding of sometimes 15 horses in training.

Also, from the City of El Reno, the City Manager Matt Sandlin and Lindsey Gragg-Mach, and her husband, a personal friend for many years.

Amanda and Nick Delore are here mingling with Betty and Leon Edwards, Sherrilynn and Jack Caster. Karen Dozier and her plus one appear to be engaged in a conversation with Eilene and Darryl Peters, who just celebrated an anniversary. I'm looking forward to an introduction to Karen's plus one. Pam Cooper and her cousin Beverly look ravishing as usual. Janice and Trish made an appearance. What fun girls.

The list goes on and on. Horsemen from reining, cutting, and even dressage. Oklahoma Cattlemen's Association and trap shooters are eager to see the improvements and anxious to know to what extent they may be able to participate.

Then, there are our friends from the NRHA, Vickie and David Lonstein of Winslow, Arkansas, Christa and Brett Leck, and you can't forget Billy Jack and Alice Rector, these two know how to make an appearance at any horsing event.

And what about the surrey, we can't omit it. No, see it's coming from the arena, and it must be a hit for they are waving. Hi! Hi, everyone! The only thing different tonight about the white fringed surrey from Doug and Amanda's wedding is the missing flowers which have been preempted by formally dressed guests. Oh yes, and bells. Can't forget the bells.

The guests staying at our cabins will be coming by any minute in a modernized version of a hayride. Bench cushioned seats, lights and, oh yes, did I say bells? I am pleased to report to you that the resort is booked into next year.

Gene DuBois is our chef extraordinaire and is cooking prime rib on the grills purchased at the Run for a Million. Hooray, no seriously they are Hooray Grills. And Chef DuBois is overseeing the opening of our expanded restaurant.

The inside is just as spectacular with garland leading to the upstairs gala event space. Lighted topiaries bring ambiance to recessed seating areas. Music, candles, and western chandeliers are welcoming all, and let's not forget the aged rafters which, once again, *hang* in anticipation of the moment (*pun intended*), and are committing to their history the revival of this legacy built by one man but now accessible to all.

The fireplace mantel displays trophies, belt buckles, and two bronze statues, one on each end. Above, on the expansive chimney, are photos of Magic and Beauty which everyone swears are the same horse but just mirrored images.

Brochures with information on both ranches' breeding and training programs, yes Amanda and Douglas are right there. Wave everyone. Well, as I was saying, information is available on the two ranches programs and even the winnings of colts sired by Magic are listed which is not only enlightening for the well versed, but educational for the novice, perhaps looking to invest or purchase.

Pete and Rosie, along with Danny and a plus one accept drinks and appetizers as they look this way.

Oh, listen. JJ is tapping his glass.

"Ladies and Gentlemen, Connie and I want to welcome you, along with State and Association dignitaries to the grand regalia for the opening of The Rocking Bar P Leisure Ranch Arena and Lodge. We sincerely hope that this will quickly turn into an event destination as we have strived to cover numerous venues not only for couple participation but families, also.

After dinner, buses will be at your disposal to give you a tour with well-versed guides to answer your questions.

Connie, would you join me up here?

Connie comes forward, wearing an after five black, off the shoulder, chemise with black Nina heels.

Before we close, by thanking each of you for coming, Connie and I want you to know by your presence at this grand event, you have made this a perfect occasion to also announce…

A hush falls over the room. Connie looks up at JJ and beams.

"Go ahead."

JJ stands with the smile of love Connie has waited to see for so long, but now is present during every eye contact the two lovers share.

"Well it seems, my future husband has become speechless. Yes, JJ and I are engaged."

The crowd erupts. Everyone comes to congratulate the couple. Connie waves to Vickie, Rosie, Amanda, Eilene, and her group of lifelong friends.

Connie struggles to keep from breaking her pledge of never letting anyone make her cry. Her vow dissolves, it seems crying is quite acceptable.

Please join us for Book four in my Seasons series, Wind of Change.

I can guarantee you one thing, Connie and JJ get married but, I, as well as you, am anxious to know where life leads these three couples.

I, also, would like to explain why "Sweet Summer Rain" didn't get published in August of 2018.

I finished "A Different Season" in August of 2016. And continued, as usual writing on "Mist of the Moment" and it was done in August of 2017. I continued, again, as usual on "Sweet Summer Rain."

And that's when my life stopped. My son, and it brings me to tears to say my son, Christopher Glen Nichols, was diagnosed with Calciphylaxis and given six months to live. Chris was at death's door for the continuous six months. His wife, Marilyn quit work to just be with him. He was in and out of the hospitals as his body fought the disease.

If you know me, I write my life. I cannot seem to write something I haven't lived. So, the following was "Sweet Summer Rain" during Chris' fight to survive. February 2018.

SWEET SUMMER RAIN

CONSTANCE LOUISE SINCLAIR

Weary and worn, I awake to the unthinkable. How could this have happened, Lord? I rise and listlessly walk the usual path, indeed the ordinary steps of life I repeat day after day. As I open the drapes and thank God for the sunshine instead of the miserable twelve-degree temperature of the last few weeks my heart screams out to God asking for understanding and for my friend as she faces the first day empty, alone and depleted.

Connie's mind reverts to the happenings of prior days where her dear friend, Rosie, with dreams unrealized, barren and lost, watched as the tiny coffin was lowered into the ground. Connie shivers and recalls as Rosie fell to her knees on the unyielding frozen earth removing her only son from her forever.

****

I do bible studies every morning and one was on Rahab and the red cord of protection she hung out her window. I said, Lord, I can do that and I hung a red ribbon in my front window.

Then I read about the woman with blood issues and her healing after touching the hem of Jesus' garment. So I placed a white ribbon with the red.

The next was Jesus Calling and the gold cord of faith and hope. I placed the gold ribbon and it curled around the red and white.

Chris called and said, "Mom, I think I'm feeling a little better today."

I told him about the ribbons as he continued to not thrive, not improve but just endure, just be. When he was sick he would be in bed. When he wasn't sick he would be up cooking, doing, and just being alive for that moment.

On September 3, 2021, Christopher Glen Nichols walked or as he said, strolled my last granddaughter to marry down the aisle in Sedgwick, Kansas. We all commented it was like a family reunion without going to a funeral. He felt remarkable. Was lively and joking, as always. Lots of pictures. Thank you, Lord, for the pictures.

The kids left for a two week honeymoon and one week to the day on September 10, 2021, Chris passed of a heart attack. I don't remember much about the funeral but I do remember the heartache of watching my only son's casket being lowered into the cold dark earth.

On a brighter note. Trey and Kelsie welcomed twins, August 23, 2022. A boy and a girl. What blessings.

Back to Sweet Summer Rain. I had the small excerpt mentioned above and that book over two-thirds done when Chris seemed to be getting better. I stopped writing, and about three years later I started another version of Sweet Summer Rain and the child lives but in real life my son doesn't.

I knew I couldn't be sad because of the blessing of my son being in my life, sooooo I took partial book one and partial book two and shuffled them together. I felt so good. So good because I could write what Chris did as a baby, like when he was asleep I could move his bed and sweep under and around him and he never woke. These parts are my healing just as Book 1, A Different Season, was my healing through Glen's passing. I can tell you that I loved Glen with my whole body and soul but when it is your child it is a whole different pain. So I thank you my dear sweet readers for letting me write for you. Your encouragement is beyond words and I am anxious to continue the series with Wind of Change.